Vengeance in Biloxi

Book Three

The Alex, Cherokee Assassin Series

James A. McGregor

Southern Sunsets Publications

Vengeance in Biloxi

Book Three
The Alex, Cherokee Assassin Series

Copyright © 2018 by James A. McGregor

www.southernsunsetspublications.com

Cover Design by Sarai Weaver

ISBN 13: 978-0-9984398-6-0

Southern Sunsets Publications

Georgetown, Florida

ACKNOWLEDGEMENTS

I could not have begun, yet finish this book without the help and inspiration of a number of people. First, my enormous gratitude to the Jacksonville Florida Baptist Heart Specialists, the Jacksonville Beach Cardiac Rehabilitation staff, and St. Augustine cardiologist Doctor Robert Kelsey, MD and his associates for keeping me on the greenside of the turf.

My thanks to numerous American Indian friends and associates for their guidance; Seth McGregor for his attention to detail and style plus his editorial skills and insights about the writer's world; Sarai Weaver for the creative work on the cover, final editing and her work with Amazon with the final publishing; my wife Christel for her endless patience and support; and to dozens of friends and associates, past and present, to business associates and dozens of acquaintances whose personalities helped create the personas of the book's characters...I hope as you find yourself and persons you know in the story, you will be pleased.

Vengeance in Biloxi

Book 3

The Alex, Cherokee Assassin Series

Author's Note

This story is part of the Alex, Cherokee Assassin fiction series and is set in the Biloxi, Mississippi area.

Insights and details for *Vengeance in Biloxi* are, in part, a result of my time spent visiting casinos throughout the southeast including numerous visits to the Biloxi area. Insights are also derived from years of work with Indian tribes and groups petitioning for federal acknowledgment. A brief discussion of these insights and the details derived from my Biloxi visits is provided here to enhance the reader's vision of the story:

A few minutes after exiting Interstate-10 onto Interstate-110 South, spectacular riverfront and beach front high rise casino hotels come into view. The first one you'll see is the beautiful new Scarlet Pearl on the north side of the Tchoutacabouffa River. Continuing on south I-110, as you cross the bridge, there are fleets of shrimp boats lining both sides of the river. Immediately to the left, on the south side of the river, is the famous Imperial Palace Casino and Hotel complex. Beyond the Imperial Palace the skyline of the high-rise casinos directly on the Gulf of Mexico are visible.

This vibrant gaming mecca consists of twelve large casinos, eleven with adjoining large hotels, lining the riverfront and gulf shore between Biloxi and Bay St. Louis. The eleven hotels provide over sixty-six hundred visitor rooms. The twelve casinos offer more than fourteen thousand slot machines and five hundred-plus table games including blackjack, roulette, and craps.

Six of the twelve are owned and operated by Wall Street based gaming and entertainment companies, the remaining six are owned by individuals and large private investment groups. The twelve include MGM's Beau Rivage, the Golden Nugget, Harrah's, and the Hard Rock. The twelve produce annual gaming revenues in excess of one billion-two hundred thousand dollars. In addition, hotel rooms along with food and beverage revenues bring the total revenues to over three billion dollars per year. The twelve enterprises combined employ over three thousand five-hundred people.

There's more. Biloxi boasts several hundred additional food and beverage facilities and hotels, miles of magnificent and accessible Gulf beaches, and a significant shrimp and fishing industry. Biloxi is also home to the Mississippi Coast Coliseum and Convention Center with its fifteen thousand person event seating capacity, and MGM Park, the six thousand seat home of the Biloxi Shuckers, a minor league baseball Double-A affiliate of the Milwaukee Brewers.

Hosting visitors is nothing new to Biloxi. Historically, Biloxi has been a favorite summer resort for over one hundred-seventy years. By the year 1850, a handful of large luxury hotels lined the beach. By 1900, the resort numbers more than doubled, and the Biloxi economy had expanded as it became the seafood capital of the world. By 1920, there were more than forty seafood factories in and near Biloxi. The shrimping and fishing industries remain an integral part of the economy, and Biloxi seafood restaurants are still famous for their great cuisine.

Biloxi and the Gulf Coast are also known for their survival of several of the strongest hurricanes in the history of the United States. Notable storms struck the area in the years 1722, 1893, 1915, and 1947, but in August 1969 Hurricane Camille dealt Biloxi a catastrophic blow.

Biloxians immediately began to rebuild; however, the economic recovery was slow. All that changed in 1992 when the State of Mississippi chose to allow legalized dockside gaming. Biloxi was on a fast path to recovery when Hurricane Katrina brought that to a standstill in 2005.

A drive on Interstate 110 plus east and west on Highway 90 confirms the miracle of the casino gaming recovery since Hurricane Katrina.

Traveling along Highway 90, the iconic Biloxi Lighthouse comes into view. The lighthouse is one of the most historic structures in the southeastern United States. The stately sixty-four foot cast iron structure beams its light signal to Gulf of Mexico mariners, shrimpers, boaters, and fishermen today just as it has for the past one hundred-seventy years. It was built while James Knox Polk was the eleventh President of the United States, and Mississippi was one of only thirty states in the United States. Technically, the fourth-order, three-on-one-off cycle uniquely identifies the lighthouse beam as Biloxi Harbor.

Biloxians speak fondly of the lighthouse as they point out to visitors that it was operated by female lighthouse keepers longer than any other lighthouse in the United States; that the light for the signal was provided by nine oil lamps from its inception in 1848 until it was electrified in 1927; and the lighthouse's amazing survival of numerous hurricanes, most recently Katrina with its nearly thirty foot seawall.

Another important symbol of the tenacity and spirit of Mississippi residents living and working along this part of the Gulf Coast is the carving of post-hurricane tree sculptures. Highway 90 is home to dozens of once beautiful live oak trees left dead by Hurricane Katrina, now transformed into sculptured work of native birds and marine life by chainsaw artist Dayton Scuggins and wood sculptor Marlin Miller.

Travel west to Bay St. Louis and find 'Angels in the Bay' created by another chainsaw sculptor, Dale K. Louis who transformed four post-hurricane live oak trees into fascinating angel creations.

Each mission in the 'Alex, Cherokee Assassin' series has four critical elements. Each takes place in a significant southeastern city, each has a casino element, each is based on an issue important to the American Indian people, and in each, Alex seeks revenge on their behalf. I find, Biloxi, Mississippi ideal as the setting for this third 'Alex, Cherokee Assassin' book.

On the eve of her first attack of this mission, Alex notes: "Four months ago I discovered Biloxi, Mississippi, a fabulous small southern city with an appalling problem. My mission is to eliminate this problem, and eliminate it effectively.

One

It's dark; it's wet; it's a bone-chilling January night in Biloxi, Mississippi. A light rain is in the air, wobbling between a mist and drizzle, just enough to make the blacktop surfaced roadway wet but not puddle. It's a damp, cold forty-four degrees Fahrenheit.

Traffic on Beach Boulevard is light. Low beam headlights focus on the roadway, providing drivers only the slightest vision of the roadsides and the tree and grass covered highway median. The Biloxi lighthouse beams faintly sharing an ill-defined light barely discernible at the roadside.

The stately sixty-four foot cast-iron lighthouse beams its light to mariners in the Gulf of Mexico through Fresnel lighthouse lenses just as it has for one hundred-seventy years. The lighthouse's plain white exterior stands out strongly in daylight from its site in the center of the Highway 90 median, but at night it is barely noticed except for its light beaming high above the roadway.

Twenty-six year old John Campbell is alone, driving on the eastbound side of the boulevard with the flat, dark sand and Gulf of Mexico on his passenger side. He stops at a red light near the base of the lighthouse. His destination is the Beau Rivage Casino Hotel for his work as a security guard. His vehicle is the third in line behind a red Ford F-150. John hears a sound outside, something like a constant screaming. The sound is barely audible over the car engine and windshield wipers. He rolls down the driver's side window a few inches, enough to hear but not let the rain inside his car. He can only see the road and the pickup truck immediately ahead. As the window opens, the muffled noise becomes a loud, irritating scream coming from the median.

It's now loud and clear. John reacts like a security guard should when curiosity is piqued. Campbell turns on his emergency lights, turns the engine off, exits his car, and then cautiously follows his flashlight's beam toward the irritating non-stop noise.

As his flashlight discovers the source, a screaming man on his knees tied to a tree, Campbell yells out: "Damn! What the hell is this? What the hell is going on here?" He slowly inches back toward his car, while pulling his cell phone from his pants pocket, and dials nine-one-one.

"I'm calling to report that there's a man tied or hooked to a tree on the boulevard. He's on his knees tied to a tree with his back to the tree. All he has on is his jockey shorts. I'm standing about eight or ten feet away and I've got my flashlight shining on him. He just keeps screaming ... non-stop screaming."

"Sir, are you on Beach Boulevard, Highway Ninety?"

"Yes, I am. I'm in the eastbound side at the stoplight near the lighthouse."

"Can you tell me if there is a street number or specific crossroad?"

"I'm just south of the lighthouse. I've got my emergency lights on."

"Thank you sir, the police have dispatched an officer. He should be there shortly."

"Okay. I'll be right here with my emergency lights on...he hasn't stopped screaming."

"Thank you again, sir. Just don't go near him. The officer is on his way."

*   *   *

"Dispatch, this is Officer Reynolds. I'm at a scene in the center of Beach Boulevard. I need backup, traffic patrol, paramedics, probably an investigator or detective. It's creepy!"

"Can you tell if he is seriously injured?" the dispatcher asks.

"I can't tell. He's tied pretty tightly to the tree," Officer Reynolds replies. "It's cold and wet. He's sopping wet. He's in his underwear. He's got to be freezing. Water is dripping off his head and chin."

"Okay, just don't touch him or let anyone else touch him," the dispatcher advises Officer Reynolds. "Paramedics and a traffic control officer are on their way. I'll send a detective A-S-A-P."

"Thanks. Hurry, this guy is on his knees, tied with his hands behind his back around the backside of a tree. All he has on is his jockey shorts and its freaking cold and raining. He just keeps screaming, no words, just a non-stop scream. I'm afraid to go close to him or touch him. I've never seen anything like this before."

"Right, Officer Reynolds. Backup is on the way."

*   *   *

When Biloxi Police Department Detective Sergeant Ronnie James and his assistant, Jan Snow, arrive at the scene they are greeted by Officer Reynolds, a traffic patrolman, and a second Biloxi Policeman. Three other non-police personnel are standing near Campbell's car. Campbell is wearing his rain gear. The rain, the cold, and the screaming continue.

Detective James walks around the screaming man for a second time. He and Jan Snow are shining their flashlights on the man. The detective shakes his head. "Miss Snow, take a lot of pictures." The detective nods to the police officers in attendance, "I need one of you officers to help me hold him up so she can get a few full shots. Be careful. He's crazed or drugged; he could bite or break loose. Just be careful."

Officer Reynolds, a second policeman, and Detective James hold the man while Officer Snow takes more photos.

"Jan, get a close shot at the two feathers stuck in his jockey shorts elastic. Okay, it looks like there's a note there too. Get a picture of the note before I remove it, then we'll take one with the message on the note."

Detective James stands from his kneeling position and looks around. By now there is a small crowd of onlookers along with the police group.

"Who found this guy?"

Officer Reynolds points to John Campbell. "This man did."

Seeing the motion, John Campbell stepped forward.

"Did you touch him?" Detective James inquires.

"No, sir. I called nine-one-one then I've just been standing at my car ever since."

"Okay, thanks."

Detective James looks around at the mixture of police officers and onlookers. "Did anybody else touch him?"

"Detective, just so you know," John Campbell says. "He's been screaming ever since I found him. I heard his scream when I stopped at the red light on my way to work. Man, just non-stop screaming."

"Okay, can you go with one of the officers and give a statement?"

"Yes, sir, I've got time. I called work and told them that I'd be late."

Detective James continues his command of the scene. "Okay, Miss Snow, finish up with any photos you might need. Paramedics, get him to the hospital. Be careful not to cut or touch any of the knots. Leave as much as you can of the straps he's tied up with just as they are. They could be important evidence. Officer Reynolds, go with the paramedics to the hospital. I'll be right behind. Meet you at the hospital."

Officer Reynolds watches the two paramedics carefully cut the straps binding the man. "Well, he finally stopped screaming. Now he's crying," He says as they carry the man to the ambulance.

*   *   *

At the lobby of the Biloxi Hospital Emergency Room, Detective Sergeant James impatiently paces while he calls the Biloxi police headquarters.

"This is Detective Sergeant James. I'm working on the case of the man found on Beach Boulevard strapped to the tree. I think you need to get someone over to 1476 Saint John's Street."

"There's some connection with this guy we found and that address. We found a note on this guy with that address on it. You might need a SWAT team. It could be dangerous. Someone who knows what they're doing tied this guy up and either tortured him, nearly scared him to death, or drugged him into some sort of insanity. I'm on my way to the Biloxi Hospital ER if anybody needs to find me."

Two

Following the early morning investigation, Detective Sergeant James drives a short distance to the MGM Park to meet with the maintenance manager. There is another ongoing case and Ronnie agreed to stop by the ballpark to see the manager and retrieve evidence in the manager's possession.

"Good to see you, Detective James. Kind of early in the morning," the manager greeted him.

"Yeah, I had to investigate a scene just down the street. I figured you might be here this early."

"When you're brought up on a farm, you get up and going early. Farmers never change," the manager said as he hands Detective James a large sealed envelope.

"Thanks again for the information, Gerald."

"Not a problem. Let me know if there's anything else I can help you with."

As Detective James turns to leave he asks, "Gerald, would you mind if I spend a few minutes out on the pitcher's mound? I used to play at *U of A*. Sometimes I just like to daydream."

"Sure, go ahead … no ballgames in January."

While Detective James is walking to the pitcher's mound he can almost hear the chant, "R J"… "R J" …"R J" … "R J" … "R J," from stands full of cheering *U of A* fans.

17

Ronnie was the team's star relief pitcher and that day long ago he was pitching to one of the best batters in the league. *U of A* leads the game five to four. The opposing team has two men on base in scoring position. It's the bottom of the ninth inning. The pitch count, two balls, two strikes. The catcher trots out to the pitcher's mound to meet with Ronnie and the first baseman. The chant gets louder and louder as they return to their positions.

"RJ"... "RJ"... "RJ"... the chant continues. Ronnie and the catcher have agreed he'll throw his version of a 'slider.' Unlike a curve ball that drops as it approaches home plate, his 'slider' appears to the batter to be a curve ball, but when Ronnie gets it right, it doesn't drop but rises sharply. The catcher needs to be ready. The batter is not likely looking for the 'slider' because Ronnie seldom throws it.

The pitch! The batter swings and misses. The pitch was perfect! *U of A* wins the game. "RJ" ... "RJ" ..."RJ" ... "R J!" fills the air of the college stadium as the *U of A* players and coaches swarm the mound jumping and gyrating in victory.

Detective James looks at his watch, then at Gerald, who is attempting to be busy with something other than looking at the detective daydreaming on the pitcher's mound. Then with a sheepish wave and grin, Ronnie walks toward the stadium exit.

Ronnie is now thirty-six. He continues to maintain his six-foot, one hundred-eighty pound outdoor tan appearance. Like so many young athletes, an injury kept him from going beyond his great performance. Ronnie was promoted to head of the detective department of the Biloxi Police Department two years ago. Four years ago he was recruited by the Biloxi Police Department to join them as a junior detective. His previous employment was with the Birmingham, Alabama Police Department where he served as a junior detective following his two year program in criminal justice at the University of Alabama, Birmingham.

His wife, Joan, is the manager of the Regions Bank branch office in Biloxi. Her career is ongoing with Regions Bank where she initially worked at their headquarters in Birmingham. She and Ronnie met while he was investigating an armed robbery of a branch bank office in Birmingham where she had been assigned during her management training program.

Ronnie, Joan, and their eight year-old daughter are accustomed to his twenty-four-seven work schedule. The long hours are nothing new, but this crime scene is like nothing he has ever seen before.

*   *   *

The seats are full in Biloxi Police Chief Gavin's office following his call for a nine o'clock in the morning meeting. Biloxi police members include Detective Sergeant Ronnie James, Police Officer Reynolds, Police Officer Doyle Hutton, Police Lieutenant Howard Bunning leader of the Biloxi Police Department SWAT Division, and Chief Gavin. The early morning event left several of the men scrambling to meet the nine o'clock hour.

Chief Gavin sits on the front edge of his desk shuffling a few sheets of paper. He looks up toward the other police officers in his office before speaking. "Okay, gentlemen, we have a briefing at ten o'clock with news reporters and a number of city officials regarding the incident, or two incidents during the night and early morning. All the audience will be curious and likely hungry for a story. I'll ask Detective Ronnie James to take the podium first, and then we can go from there. I expect we'll have a number of questions regarding the man found tied to the tree and regarding the SWAT operations. I'll ask Detective James to cover those questions regarding the first incident then have Lieutenant Bunning to be available to handle questions regarding the SWAT operations."

Chief Gavin looks back at the notes in his hands and continues. "I'll take questions regarding where the cases are now, and what they can expect going forward. Let's be careful to stick to a brief outline for this presentation and questions. As always, feel free to keep certain details to yourself whenever you believe it's necessary. We're just at the beginning of the investigation. Ronnie, give us a quick look at the first guy, where are we with him?"

Detective James stands up and walks over to Chief Gavin's desk. "Well, Chief, the man is still in a stupor. He comes across as terrified. We don't know who he is or who strapped him to the tree. He's currently in protective custody. A psychiatrist has examined him briefly to figure out what's wrong with him; so far the medical doctors haven't found any drugs in his system. He hasn't stopped shaking. We've taken prints to see if we can find out who he is. We do know he is likely connected in some way to the house with the women and the pimp, so we'll be working with them to see if they can or will identify him."

Detective James steps back and hesitates before continuing. "There are some things like the way he was strapped to the tree. It's hard to figure out how it was done, why it was done or who did it. There's the fact he was tied up with leather or sinew straps, not rope, not duct tape ... not zip ties ... but leather straps. I'll ask that we don't let this fact leave this room. Okay, Chief. That's it."

"Thanks Ronnie." Chief Gavin says. "That sounds good, but we should try to keep the phrase 'pimp' out of our discussion with the press and city officials. The press might go nuts and we don't know for sure. I agree with you, detective. Let's keep the details you mentioned to those of us in this room. Okay, next, Lieutenant Bunning, let's hear from you on the SWAT operation."

Lieutenant Bunning served in the Army Special Forces for five years during the Afghanistan War before returning to his home in Louisiana. He has been an officer with the Biloxi Police Department for the past four years. He is wearing his on-duty SWAT camouflage uniform.

"Thanks, Chief. I'll be brief. Well, as you all know, we had an early morning call for an operation not far from here based on a tip from Detective James regarding the man they found bound to the tree. Our SWAT team members surrounded the two-story house at 1476 Saint John's Street. The house was totally dark, no lights on. We approached the main entrance, the front door, identified ourselves and demanded they open it. Still no lights and no response. We waited two minutes with no response and then we used a ram to break open the door. A man exited a side door and was immediately apprehended by one of our SWAT team. He and two of the young women had ID in their possession; the man had a cell phone. Inside the house we found a total of six women who were taken into custody. All were given their rights and taken to headquarters for questioning. At that time they were turned over to the Biloxi police and detectives."

"Thanks, Lieutenant Bunning and Detective James, any questions?" Chief Gavin asked as he looked around the room.

"We have the man's cell phone. I believe it's a burner phone," adds Detective James. "We're attempting to follow up on the few calls he made with it."

"If there are no more questions, let's get over to the briefing room," says Chief Gavin as he stands up from his desk.

*   *   *

A rare standing room only crowd is assembled for the ten-o'clock briefing regarding a complex and unusual pair of related events. Two members of the Biloxi City Council, the president of the Biloxi Chamber of Commerce, and the mayor are in attendance along with the Biloxi Chief of Police, numerous other senior Biloxi police officers, and members of the press and media.

"Good Morning. I'm Biloxi Chief of Police, Bryan Gavin. Earlier this morning members of the Biloxi police department were called to a scene on Highway 90, Beach Boulevard, involving one male, apparently in serious distress. This led to a second event on Saint John's Street involving a second man and six young women. Biloxi Police Department Detective Sergeant Ronnie James was called to the scene of the first event. He has been assigned to head the investigation of the two events. I'll now call on Detective James to brief you on this. Please hold any questions until he is through with his briefing."

"Thanks Chief Gavin," Detective James said taking the podium. He turns to face the audience. "I'm Detective Sergeant Ronnie James of the Biloxi Police Department. Chief Gavin has assigned me to be the lead detective in this case and the case of the subsequent discovery of six young women and one other man found in a house on Saint John's Street."

Detective James continues, "The man bound to the tree was discovered at approximately three-twenty this morning by a man traveling east on Beach Boulevard. The man bound to the tree was found wearing only a pair of jockey shorts. He was found on his knees with his ankles and upper arms tied together behind his back around the tree. He had a note with the Saint John's Street address tucked in the elastic of his Jockey shorts. He was conscious, screaming loudly, but could not speak coherently, just screaming gibberish. He was taken to the emergency room where he remains in custody under medical observation with two Biloxi police officers guarding him."

Detective James takes a break from his notes and opens up a second file before continuing. "After finding the note attached to the bound man, I called our headquarters and asked that they send a SWAT team to the Saint John's Street address written on the note. At approximately five-fifteen this morning they surrounded the house, called for someone to come out to meet with the police. When there was no response, they used a ram to gain entrance to the two-story house. There, they discovered and apprehended a man and six young women, ranging from age fifteen to nineteen. Two were carrying identification; the others claim to have identification left in the house. We have not yet recovered all of the identification. All eight people, the first man found and the seven persons found in the house, are in custody. The first man found and the six women are being examined at the Biloxi Medical Center. The second man, the man found at the house, is in custody at the Biloxi police department for questioning. He was carrying identification including a Louisiana driver's license which we're attempting to confirm. We're also attempting to confirm the ownership of the Cadillac Escalade found at the Saint John's Street house. The suspect did have an unregistered cell phone in his possession. We're actively following up on the numbers that he had called from that phone."

As Detective James looks up from his notes and at Chief Gavin, Police Chief Gavin approaches the podium and speaks. "I believe we have time for a few questions, but please be brief. We have a lot of work to do on this case. We'll try to keep you informed with another briefing later today or around this time tomorrow morning."

"Detective James, you said the man was tied with his back to a tree?" Asks a reporter, "And, do you know how he got there?"

"Yes, he was on his knees, bound with straps with his back to the tree. And, no, we do not know how he got there. He has not been coherent enough to communicate. We do not know who he is. There was no wallet or identifying items found. We will continue to attempt to identify him through fingerprints and other methods until he becomes coherent. We're searching records statewide to see if anyone else has ever been found bound and tied like this."

"Do you know if this is gang related?" drawled a seasoned Biloxi news reporter.

Detective James turns to the reporter and replies, "No, we do not know at this time, but we will determine if it is as the investigation continues."

A member of the Biloxi City Council stands and speaks. "Detective James, do you know, or do you suspect this involves prostitution?"

"Again, we don't know, but we will determine if it does as the investigation continues."

Detective James steps back from the podium and looks over at Chief Gavin. "Chief, I'd like to end the briefing until we have more time to work on this."

"We'll take one more question," Chief Gavin announces.

"Detective, was the first man beaten or injured? And what about the others, were they injured?"

Detective James turns to face the reporter. "The first man appears to be traumatized... so far he can't speak. He does not appear to have been beaten, and according to the medical examiners there were no drugs detected in his system at this point in time. I don't have any such information regarding the persons found in the Saint James Street house."

"Detective James, is the tree he was tied to one of the Marlin Miller carvings?" asks a hotel security chief seated in the audience.

"Yes. He was tied to the trunk of what is called the eagle tree."

"Do you know if there is any symbolism involved in using this tree?" The security chief persists.

"Okay, I'll take this as the last question. At this point, no, it's too early to speculate about things like that," Detective James replies.

Detective James looks around the crowded room. "Just for clarification, the so-called 'eagle tree' is one of several trees left dead by Hurricane Katrina. An artist named Marlin Miller with funding from the City of Biloxi carved figures on the branches of these trees. The one just west of the lighthouse near the westbound lane has a large eagle carved into an extended branch. That's where the man was found … bound to the trunk at the base of that tree."

A man from the audience stands and says, "Sir, I'm a member of the Biloxi Tourist Council. May I offer some clarification on the eagle tree?"

"Yes, please do."

"The particular eagle tree you are referring to is near the lighthouse. There is a more prominent eagle tree west of Biloxi at Pass Christian and there is a third one, I believe, somewhat smaller, somewhere between the two. All three are along Highway 90."

"Thank you sir. All right, let's call an end to this session." Chief Gavin interrupts. "Thank you all for being here."

A member of the Biloxi Chamber of Commerce asks, "Chief Gavin, when do you expect to have another update?"

"When we have further information," Chief Gavin replies. "We're really just beginning our work on this. Again, thank you all for being here this morning."

Three

Surveillance of money drop locations and delivery routines is a cornerstone of preparation for a mission where money derived from illegal activities is an element. Alex's years of training and experience in the importance of 'following the money' plays a major part of this mission's success or failure. During the four months of preparation and work with this mission her focus, learning everything possible about their money trail had been a key to success. Two nights ago Alex stalked the first victim of this mission from his delivery to the designated money drop location. Her attack on the man was late that night following his delivery of young women captives to a hotel.

*   *   *

Alex is at the site of one of the four nests she has discovered. It's four o'clock in the afternoon. A man carrying a small backpack enters the SUV parked in the driveway, right on time. As he goes into the motion of fastening his seatbelt, Alex jumps from her crouched position on the rear floor behind the front passenger seat. As the startled man turns toward Alex, she places her hand blow reed to her lips and with a strong blow, delivers the powder rendering the man unconscious seconds later.

*   *   *

Twenty-six year old Grayson Branch is driving his 2008 Toyota Tacoma pickup truck east on Highway 90.

The five and one-half mile route from his Biloxi apartment to his work as a blackjack dealer at Boomtown Casino follows his three-hour study at Crescent School of Gaming and Bartending in Gulfport, a fifteen minute drive the other direction, west on Highway 90.

Grayson's two week old routine is his effort to expand his career opportunity and horizons in the Biloxi casino and hotel industry. Grayson shares an apartment with Joyce Lee, a bartender at the Hard Rock Casino and Hotel complex.

Tonight, his travel to work is routine. The pickup truck heater is on, and his Alan Jackson CD is playing. He arrives at Boomtown at seven twenty-six p.m. and parks his pickup in the back row of the employee designated Boomtown. The evening is colder than usual, no rain, but a heavy cast of dark clouds. He grabs his hooded sweatshirt as he slides out of his driver's seat then hurries through the parking area to the main casino entrance. Once inside, he works his way to the employee area to sign in and prepare for work.

Nearly three hours later, Boomtown employee, Phyllis Movalson, rushes into the main entrance of the casino and anxiously advises the security officer at the main entrance:

"Mike, there's a person in the back of a pickup truck in the employee parking area. He's just lying there. I don't think he has any shirt or jacket on. It's freezing outside. We need to get a security guard out there right away."

Mike quickly grabs his two way radio. "Security station, it's Mike at the main entrance. One of our employees just came in and she's reporting a person or a body in the bed of a pickup truck in the employee parking area. We need to get someone out there right away."

Mike turns to Miss Movalson. "We have a patrol car out there. Exactly where is the truck?"

Phyllis Movalson speaks loudly as though talking to the parking lot patrolman via the two way radio. "All the way back in the employee area, it's right next to my red Ford Fusion. All I know is it's a pickup truck."

The parking lot patrolman turns on the emergency lights and accelerates his vehicle quickly to the rear of the lot.

"Okay, I think this is it." He turns his flashlight on and inches his way to the vehicle. "Holy shit! She's right. There's a body...call the chief. I'll wait here."

The patrolman walks to the other side of the pickup. "Make sure you remind him it's cold as the North Pole out here. I'm looking at this guy. He doesn't have a shirt or anything on top. No jacket, nothing. Hey, it looks like money in his underwear and his pants pockets ... money just sticking out." The patrolman pauses, aims his flashlight the length of the man's body. "He's not moving...he's either dead or passed out...got to be freezing."

Flashing yellow emergency lights illuminate the parking area. A long eight minutes after the call from Boomtown Casino Security, two Biloxi police cars arrive from opposite directions, each one with lights flashing and sirens blaring. The ambulance is immediately behind the second police car, lights and sirens full blast. The two police officers and two paramedics join the Boomtown security.

The first paramedic jumps into the back of the pickup and gently moves the body. "He's still alive. I need a thermal blanket. We need to move him very carefully. Damn, he's tied up," he says as he begins to place a blanket over the man. "What the hell! His arms and legs are all tied up. Man, he really stinks," he says, shaking his head back-and-forth, while looking at the man.

Biloxi Police Officer Ken Reynolds looks at the unconscious man lying on the metal floor of the pickup truck. "Is he tied with his arms and legs tied behind his back?"

"Yes, sir, he is," replies the paramedic.

"Okay, that's similar to last night. Can you move him without untying him?"

The paramedic hesitates and turns the body carefully. "No, I think we need to cut these strips then get him to the emergency room right away."

"Okay, give me a second. Let me help you cut the straps," responds Officer Reynolds. "The detective will want to see them as intact as possible. He was really focused...actually pretty obsessed with that last night."

Police Officer Reynolds speaks into his two way radio. "Headquarters, this is Officer Reynolds. I'm at the Boomtown Casino scene. We have a man, unconscious, tied up like the man last night. Paramedics are en route to the hospital emergency room with him. I'm sure Detective James will want to see him. We cut the straps he's tied up with but left them on him."

"Roger, Officer Reynolds," Headquarters replies. "We'll contact Detective James. I just got off the phone with Boomtown Security. I'll go ahead and make arrangements to impound the car or truck he was in. I'll get back in touch with Boomtown Security. Officer, who is the other police officer with you?"

"Officer Dean."

"Can you have him stay with the pickup 'til they impound it?"

"I'll take care of that." Officer Reynolds states emphatically.

"Okay. When they called in it looks like they said the lady who found the man and the driver of the pickup truck are both being held by Boomtown security. Officer Reynolds, can you join the other officer and the Boomtown Security people?" The headquarters officer pauses, and then continues. "Yeah, the notes here do say we were advised that there are two witnesses or persons involved."

"Roger," replies Officer Reynolds as he walks over to talk to Officer Dean.

*   *   *

Officer Reynolds joins Officer Dean, the head of Boomtown security, Phyllis Movalson, and Grayson Branch in the casino security office.

John Farley, head of Boomtown Security introduces himself to Officer Reynolds and advises him that he and a third Biloxi Police Officer, Josh Carlson, have begun to take statements made by Miss Movalson and Mr. Branch. The conversation continues:

"Thanks Mr. Farley and Officer Carlson for taking care of that," says Officer Reynolds. "I believe Detective James will want to speak with Miss Movalson and Mr. Branch, likely sometime later tonight or in the morning."

He continues, turning to Grayson Branch. "Mr. Branch, the police are going to impound your vehicle, so you'll have to get other transportation. I'll check with headquarters to see if it's okay to go back to your job."

Officer Reynolds steps out of the security office to make a call. "Headquarters, its Officer Reynolds. I'm with Boomtown security and the persons involved in finding the man in the back of the pickup truck. Please advise if it's okay to release them from the Boomtown security office."

"Roger, Officer Reynolds. Let's hold them there 'til we contact Detective James. He'll probably want to talk to them first."

*   *   *

A Biloxi police officer is guarding the intensive care hospital room where the man from the back end of the pickup truck is being tended by a hospital nurse.

The police officer greets Detective James. "Sir, go ahead in. The nurse is here."

Detective James addresses the nurse with a slight nod of his head. "Hi, I'm Detective James. I'm here to see how this man is doing."

"I'm Barbara Kline. He's not well. He's basically comatose; possibly in shock from the cold. We're not sure. We're waiting for the results from blood tests for drugs. I've been assigned to be with him until I'm told otherwise."

The nurse retrieves a clear plastic bag and hands it to the detective. "These items were in his pockets...the feathers were stuck in the elastic of his underwear along with several dollar bills; twenties, fifties …. Your police officers have an accounting of the money."

"He does look rough. Anything from the doctors?"

"Nothing yet."

"The police officer gave us instructions to leave the straps tied until you have looked at them," she said motioning towards the man on the bed.

"Yes, thanks for leaving them on."

Detective James looks carefully at each knot. "Nurse Kline, Ma'am, can you help me turn him over so I can see his back?"

Once he is turned over, Detective James takes his time searching the man's backside. "Okay, ma'am, can you get me a pair of sharp scissors to cut these straps off him?"

Nurse Kline picks up the scissors and sternly replies, "Sir, I can't let you do it. Just show me where you want me to cut the straps."

As they coordinate the cutting and removal of the straps, Nurse Kline notes, "Detective, these straps are leather. It seems strange."

"Yes, Miss Kline. It is," Detective James replies. "Thanks for your help. And let the officer outside know if there are any changes."

Detective James leaves the room and turns to the officer outside. "Officer, please give me a call as soon as he's conscious."

*   *   *

"Chief Gavin, it is Detective Ronnie James. Sorry to call you at this hour. It looks like we have another case of a man being bound, hogtied, and stripped of everything except his pants. This time he was found in the back end of a pickup truck parked in the Boomtown Casino parking lot."

"What the hell!"

"Chief, I'm just leaving the hospital where he is being treated. He's unconscious. He has a wallet and driver's license with a Biloxi address ... yeah, and like last night, a note with an address stuck in the elastic of his underwear. I'd like to get the SWAT team over there. "

"Okay, detective, I'll call it in and have them contact you for the address."

"Chief, another thing, the man had money ... a number of dollar bills stuck in his underwear. He also had the identification of two young women in his pockets."

"Okay, detective, call me when you need to. Let's plan on getting together at seven o'clock tomorrow morning. We'll have the media and the mayor's office and who–knows-who all calling," the Chief said grimly.

*   *   *

Chief Gavin speaks while rubbing his chin: "Ronnie, I know you've had a long night again. Help me get a grip on this so we can get the help we need to figure this all out before we deal with the media and mayor's office."

"Well Chief, we've made some progress on the first case. The women are all alive and appear to be okay, but they're young, abused, and traumatized. It looks like they've been brought here from out of town. We have them in protective custody and are providing them with medical attention and counseling. We have personnel attempting to get in touch with their families ... to get them taken care of."

"Good. I see there's a report on my desk and one in my e-mail. They should provide details. What about the first man, the one tied to the tree and the other guy the SWAT team found in the house?"

"The man tied to the tree is still out of it. He's alive and apparently medically okay, but he's still unable to speak. He can't tell us his name. He's in isolation at the hospital. The women haven't identified him by name, just that they know he was a part of their capture and use."

"We've identified the second guy. He's lawyered up, but the women have described him as the one who is in control of the whole thing. From what little we've learned, both men were likely involved in the recruiting or kidnapping of these women. We believe there are four women from Mississippi and two from other states."

Chief Gavin replies, shaking his head, "Crap, Ronnie, that's interstate. The feds can and most likely will get involved...interstate trafficking."+

Chief Gavin stands up from his desk and takes a few steps. "Detective, I need to get the city attorney involved." The Chief presses intercom button. "Viola, can you get hold of Mark at the city attorney's office. Put him through to me when you do. Thanks."

"Okay, so, Ronnie, let's get to last night's event."

"For starters, Chief, the man was tied up the same way as the man tied to the eagle tree, just without the tree. He was found in the back end of a pickup truck parked at the rear of the Boomtown parking lot. Like the first man, he appears to be traumatized or drugged, more like a coma. He's pretty beat up, could be from being bounced around in the back end of the open pickup. His mouth is cut and a few of his front teeth are broken. Being in a coma, he can't speak. He was damn-near dead when the paramedics arrived and took him to the hospital."

Detective James pauses, then continues. "We believe he was in the back end of the pickup, wide open, no cover, nothing for at least three hours, maybe more. The other thing, Chief, he had quite a bit of money ... bundles of twenty and fifty dollar bills tucked in his pants pockets and underwear elastic."

"So, whoever did this to him didn't take or need the money." The chief replies. "And you said you saw him late last night?"

"Yes, sir, actually early this morning. He was in the emergency room, but I believe they were planning to move him to intensive care. This guy had pants on, but no shirt, no shoes, no undershirt; just bare from the belt up."

The intercom interrupts. Viola's voice chimes in, "Chief, Mark from the city attorney's office is on the line."

"Thanks, Viola."

"Mark, Chief Gavin here. Is it possible for you to come over to my office? We've got an emergency that needs your attention."

Attorney Mark Acres voice comes through strongly over the intercom. "Sure, Chief. Give me twenty minutes. I've got something first, and then I'll be on my way. Is this about the prostitutes?"

"Yes, it is. But I'm afraid it's more complicated than that. Detective James is here with me, we'll give you all the details when you get here."

"Chief, I'll see you soon."

Chief Gavin looks up from his intercom and swivels his chair to turn back to Detective James. "Okay, Ronnie, let's continue with the second episode."

"We found the man's wallet, or some man's wallet, plus identification for two young women in his pants pocket. We also found the money I mentioned before, quite a bit of money. We found two feathers stuck in his underwear elastic...like the first guy. The ID in his wallet has a Biloxi address, the same address as the note tucked in the elastic of his underwear."

"We sent the SWAT team to that address. They arrested another man and five young women at that house. All six are in custody. I was told the women are, or will be, examined by medical personnel. The IDs of two women were found in the tied up man's pockets, but the two women have not been found."

"So that's possibly seven."

"More likely than possibly,"

"It looks like we have our hands full, Ronnie. Are there any suspects as to who is capturing the men, tying them up, bringing them to everyone's attention? Could it be vigilante justice?"

"Chief, there are a handful of things I'm beginning to focus on. First, the feathers, there's some message there. Second, the two men are tied up the same way...identical leather or sinew straps ... not rope or twine, but three-eighth inch soft leather straps. Third, the way the arms and legs were tied or strapped are identical, and the knots are identical. The knots are perfect square knots; right-over-left, left-over-right, all the same tightness. They're all identical."

"Any ideas?"

"There has to be two or more persons doing this ... and, they have to be fairly strong, physically. I believe, too, that they might be professionals. This isn't just two guys leaving the bar, going after someone. They know their targets and they're good at what they do. The drugs or whatever they have used to knock these guys out is a mystery to everyone, especially the doctors and nurses. No drugs have been detected in their systems."

"I wonder, Ronnie. Could it be retaliation for one or more of the women who have been found?"

"It's possible, Chief. Found or rescued."

The two are interrupted by an intercom message that City Attorney Mark Acres has arrived.

Four

"Mark, how are you?" Chief Gavin welcomes Attorney Acres and then introduces Detective James to him. Detective James gives Attorney Acres the same rundown of the events to date while Chief Gavin listens.

Following the briefing, Attorney Acres responds. "So, I've read all the notes that have crossed my desk, and I've heard all the rumors and scuttlebutt. It appears we have our hands full, the idea of the possible kidnapping, transporting, and trafficking of young women across state lines scares the hell out of me."

"Me too, Mark," agreed the Chief.

"Chief, have you talked to the mayor today?" asks Attorney Acres.

"Not today. He and his office have been briefed on the first event, but we haven't talked yet today regarding the second. The topic of sex trafficking across state lines just came up this morning."

"Chief, let's get him on the phone and schedule a time to meet with him right away," suggests Attorney Acres.

Chief Gavin rubs his chin before speaking. "I agree."

Attorney Acres stands up abruptly before announcing. "Let me get one of my assistants over here right away to take notes and so forth. We've got to be very careful with this."

*   *   *

Following the arrival and introduction of city attorney's assistant, Ann Clee, Attorney Acres says, "Okay, let's continue. We need to be prepared when we meet with Mayor Williams. Let's get into the details of this situation."

"Ronnie, give us an overview first then get into more of the details," directs Chief Gavin.

Detective James sits up straight in his seat and looks at each in the eye. "We suddenly have eleven victims of what is likely sex trafficking, and interstate sex trafficking, plus we believe two more are missing or at large. We have four men involved, two were bound, one tied to the eagle tree, the other in the back end of a pickup truck. Both are comatose or hallucinating from some sort of drug or unknown treatment, the other two men are coherent and in custody. One of them has lawyered up. There are numerous medical personnel involved with examining the women and two comatose men. The other factor, someone bound the two men and tied one to a tree, and threw the other one in the back of the pickup truck of an unsuspecting person; we believe the pickup truck driver doesn't know anything about how the man got there. And, we don't have any suspect or suspects as to who did this or why."

Chief Gavin nods and speaks, "Mark, I believe detective James summed this up very well."

Attorney Acres shakes his head. "Well, let's get a plan together for our discussion with the mayor."

He shakes his head again as he pauses and gathers his notes. "First, let's look at interstate sex trafficking. I'll get in touch with the state attorney general, then he and I can determine who to approach for advice among the state and federal agencies."

Attorney Acres continues. "Second, Detective James, for your interrogation of all these people, the four male trafficking suspects and the eleven possibly thirteen women, you'll have to be sure that each one is offered legal representation. How involved are the public defender's office and the prosecuting attorney's offices?"

Chief Gavin advises, "I believe all of the people involved in the first incident have been assigned legal representation. We're just getting started on those involved in last night's incident. We'll need to include the public defender's office and the prosecuting attorney."

Detective James nods positively then speaks. "Mr. Acres, one of the men, the coherent one, from the first night has lawyered up. I haven't heard about the coherent one from the second night. The incoherent one from the first night has been assigned an attorney and the same will be for the incoherent man from last night. I don't know if any of the women has named an attorney."

Chief Gavin adds, "Another issue, Mark, we have someone attacking these men, tying them up, putting them on display, and guiding us to houses filled with sex slaves. We haven't developed a confident profile of who is doing this, and we don't have any specific evidence. Ronnie, Is that correct?"

Detective James once again sits up, moves to the front of his chair and speaks. "There are a number of items of evidence found consistent with both men. Each one appears to have been drugged or mentally traumatized, but medical professionals haven't found any trace of drugs on the first man after a significant testing. Each man was bound, tied up, strapped with identical leather straps, tied in an identical way; arms tied immediately above the elbows then drawn behind the back; legs tied at the ankles then drawn together with knees bent behind the back, then the two, arms and legs, drawn together. Each knot is identical. Each man was tied up using nine knots. Every one of the eighteen knots is an identical perfect square knot … right-over-left, left-over-right."

Detective James pauses, sits back in his chair, and then continues. "There's more. Each man had two or three feathers, possibly seagull feathers, tucked into the elastic of his underwear. Each man was without most of his clothing exposing him to cold and raining weather. Each man had a note in the elastic of their underwear. Both notes provided us with an address where young women were being kept. We suspect and believe these women were being held hostage as sex slaves. There is one item with the second man that's different. The second man had several twenty and fifty dollar bills stuffed in his pants pockets and underwear elastic. That eliminates robbery or stealing money from the pimps. So, Mr. Acres, we have a number of bits of evidence, but so far they don't add up to provide us with a profile of the person doing this."

Attorney Acres gazes around the room thoughtfully and then speculates, "If this is a vendetta, it should show up in the saving of the young women or one group or gang of sex traffickers getting even with the other or attempting to eliminate the others … but the money?" Attorney Acres pauses and looks directly at the chief and Detective James and says, "I suggest we profile the young women and the four men and see if there are any answers there."

"Ronnie, what do you think?" Chief Gavin asks.

"I agree. We have them all in custody so this is a good time."

Chief Gavin turns toward the two men. "I think the best people to do this with the young women will be their counselors. My guess is that they have already done much of that with the women involved in the first incident. I'll take care of it. I've worked before with the two female counselors in charge. Mark and Ronnie, I believe we should have the prosecuting attorney's office look into that with the four men."

Each mumbles an agreement.

Chief Gavin stands up and says, "Okay, I think now is a good time to call the mayor and advise him of where we are with this and what we're doing. Let's schedule a meeting with him later today to discuss how we intend to address the situation."

Attorney Acres nods, "I agree, advise him of what we're doing, don't ask for permission. Yeah, Chief, go ahead and make the call."

Chief Gavin speaks into his office intercom, "Viola, can you get the mayor on the phone and forward the call to me?"

*   *   *

Mayor Williams returns the call almost immediately.

The mayor speaks in a hurried tone. "Chief, thank heavens you called. I'm being bombarded with calls and messages regarding this prostitution news. What's going on?"

"Mayor Williams, I'm in my office with Attorney Acres and the lead detective on these cases. I have you on speaker-phone."

"That's fine, Chief. Thanks to all three of you for being there."

Chief Gavin continues, "We've been in conference discussing the two episodes putting all the pieces together. We've determined its most likely sex trafficking involving young women victims, some brought here from other states."

Mayor Williams speaks quickly in response, "So, what does all that mean?"

The three men in Chief Gavin's office pause and then Chief Gavin nods to Attorney Acres. Mark Acres speaks, "Well, it's not good. We're having discussions with the prosecuting attorney's office, the public defender's office and counselors who are working with the young women. Then it will involve others."

"Mayor Williams, we're doing what we can to ascertain where these women are from. If we know or believe they have been brought here from other states we'll need to notify federal and state officials, most likely get them involved. Chief Gavin, Detective James and I will know soon if, and how many are under the age of sixteen and have been brought in... either kidnapped or lured."

Mayor Williams asks, "What do you recommend I tell the city council members, the press and all the others?"

Attorney Acres pauses then replies. "I recommend you advise them that we'll have information available late this afternoon; that you have been in touch with the Chief, the lead detective and myself; that you are meeting with them sometime after one o'clock this afternoon; and that we'll have a briefing later today, possibly tomorrow. And, Sir, I'd keep the topic of sex trafficking and young women being brought in from other states out of the conversations for now. If we find it's true, we can bring it out at that time."

Mayor Williams says hurriedly, "I've just been handed a note that Lieutenant Governor Shannessy is on hold."

Attorney Acres responds, "I would tell him just what I said. And, Mayor, if the lieutenant governor wants to talk to me, I'll be glad to take his call."

*   *   *

At two o'clock in the afternoon, the following press release is issued to the officials of the local press and City of Biloxi officials:

"A briefing and press conference will be held at the Biloxi, Mississippi City Hall Chambers at ten o'clock the morning of January 22, 2017 to discuss the current situation regarding the discovery of a number of men and women now held in custody and their possible involvement in prostitution."

What was not announced or included in the published press release is that there will be state and federal officials attending, in addition to the mayor, city officials and police officials. Attorney Acres and Mayor Williams will spend the remainder of the day and evening contacting numerous local, state, and federal offices and officials and apprising them of the situation.

Five

A large and intense overflow crowd is assembled in the forty-two seat facility for the ten o'clock morning meeting. The cold and damp drizzle has resulted in an abundance of raincoats, winter coats, sweaters, umbrellas, hats and cold-weather scarves to be placed onto two piles on side tables and attendee's arms and laps. The musty scent of wet wool and garments recently harvested from closets and storage to combat the cold wet Biloxi January winter fills the air in the room.

Local attendees include Biloxi City Council members, representatives of local casino and hotel operators and security members, representatives from the Biloxi Chamber of Commerce and numerous media personnel. Representatives of the local public defender's and prosecuting attorney's offices are also in the audience. Out of town attendees include the Mississippi Assistant State Attorney General and an assistant to the Mississippi Lieutenant Governor. Biloxi City Attorney Acres stands at the podium with Biloxi Police Chief Gavin and Mayor Williams on either side.

City Attorney Acres addresses the crowd. "Ladies and gentlemen, thank you all for being here. I'm Biloxi City Attorney Mark Acres. To my left is Biloxi Mayor Mike Williams and to my right is Biloxi Chief of Police Bryan Gavin," as he nods to each. "I'll get right to the point of this meeting. We have been confronted with a very serious situation involving eleven young women and four men who, we believe, are involved in prostitution in Biloxi. The situation likely involves the men controlling and using the young women as sex slaves for prostitution. The issue of kidnapping and the sex trafficking of these women from Mississippi and from other states is likely."

"The situation is further complicated by how it has been discovered. Two of the four men we have in custody were found bound and partially clothed, one tied to a tree, the other found in the back of a pickup truck. Each of the men had been drugged or traumatized to the extent that they were, and remain, incapable of communicating in any way. Each man had a note attached to his clothing with the address of houses in Biloxi where police from the Biloxi Police Department SWAT team, led by Lieutenant Howard Bunning, found and captured one other man in each house, plus five women in one house, six in the other. We have reason to believe there are two other additional women who have not yet been found."

"We have contacted and requested help and assistance from the Mississippi State Attorney General, the Federal Bureau of Investigation, and the Mississippi Bureau of Investigation, along with local and state officials in surrounding counties. We have also held briefings with local casino and hotel security officers and officials."

Mark pauses as he glances around the room. "The four men are in Biloxi Police custody. Three have been identified, the fourth is still unknown. He was found without identification and he remains unable to communicate. The men and women involved have not been able to, or have refused to positively identify him. The eleven women are currently in the custody and care of a local medical facility and are working with senior medical counselors. At this time, the person or persons who captured and bound the two men have yet to be identified, and at this point the police do not have any suspects, specific or otherwise."

Attorney Acres pauses again and slowly takes two sips of water before looking around the room and continuing. "We ask that each of you ask your associates to provide the Biloxi Police Department with any information regarding these situations, and certainly advise the police of any known or suspected situations regarding prostitution and sex trafficking. With that, we at the city attorney's office and mayor's office, and the Biloxi police department will continue to work with numerous state and local officials and provide you with updates as we see necessary."

A local news reporter in the audience stands and says, "Sir, this appears to be a sudden revelation...the idea of several young women prostitutes in Biloxi. It seems that this should have been known to the police before this."

Chief Gavin steps forward and responds, "Sir, we are an effective police department. There are over six thousand six-hundred casino hotel rooms in the Biloxi area. When you include all the other hotels, bed and breakfasts and other visitor rental units it's over nine thousand. In addition, our population has grown to over fifty-five thousand people. The casinos and hotels employ over three thousand five-hundred people. They have to travel on our Biloxi roads to get to and from work. Our average number of visitors is over ten thousand each day ... and when there's a major event at the Coliseum and Convention Center, add another ten to fifteen thousand. That's just vehicle traffic. In addition, last year our police department handled an average of over twenty-five hundred incident reports per week."

Chief Gavin pauses, steps to the side of the podium, then back to the microphone. He continues, "With that in mind, our Biloxi police officer staff is fewer than one hundred-fifty people. That's what we have to provide police services twenty-four hours a day, seven days a week."

Chief Gavin pauses again and turns to face the reporter. "Sir, prostitution arrests are a constant and ongoing function of our police department. We also get a great deal of help policing prostitution from several of the casino and hotel security departments. What's going on with these young women is something different. It's sex slavery, not street prostitution. The men controlling these young women are professionals."

Another media reporter stands and speaks. "Chief, is what you're saying, these women are victims, not prostitutes?"

Chief Gavin replies again. "Yes, that's what we believe. Our investigation and questioning of the women and two men who are coherent is ongoing. But, yes, that's what we believe."

The first reporter stands again. "Then, Chief, are the young women under suspicion or under arrest?"

Attorney Acres quickly steps alongside Chief Gavin. "Chief, let me respond," addressing the reporter he continued, "The eleven women are in custody being detained as potential witnesses while receiving medical treatment. They are being questioned as to how they got here, where they're from and so forth. They are not under arrest. The men are being held for suspicion of solicitation and sex trafficking, as well as the interstate trafficking of these women. They are being questioned by local, state, and federal authorities."

A well-dressed lady in the front row of the audience immediately stands, and in a strong voice, speaks as she turns to the audience. "Attorney Acres, may I speak for a moment?"

She continues without waiting for a response from Attorney Acres. "My name is Mazie Rossell. I am a Louisiana attorney and I represent a Louisiana Indian tribe and two of the eleven young women victims you have in custody are members of that tribe. Six of the young women you have in custody are Native American, and I ask at this time to represent all six until each one has her own attorney."

Attorney Acres responds. "The public defender's office has already provided each of the eleven with council. I suggest you meet with the public defender's office following this meeting."

Attorney Rossell continues, still facing the audience. "Yes, I will do that. But it's my understanding that they are not under arrest. I'm concerned about their rights being violated. To all of you attending today, if I can have a few more minutes, perhaps I can shed some light on what appears to be happening here. First, more than half of the young women victims, six of the eleven, have been identified as Native American. The six are believed to be from three southeastern states; Mississippi, Louisiana, and Alabama. Native American leaders are plagued with how and why our beautiful, wonderful, young women are vulnerable to being recruited into sex slavery..."

Mark Acres interrupts, "Attorney Rossell, perhaps..."

From the audience, the Mississippi Assistant State Attorney General stands and speaks. "Attorney Acres, I'd like to hear what else she has to say."

The sound of several muffled voices and sight of several heads nodding in agreement leaves the door open for Mrs. Rossell to continue.

"Thank you. I am very appreciative," Mrs. Rossell says with a nod to the Assistant Attorney General. "Our young people see so many other young Americans with nice clothing, jewelry, cell phones, laptop computers, cars, living in nice homes while they go without. Young women as young as fourteen years old are either recruited, lured, or forced into uncompromising situations, taken from their homes and homelands, savagely raped then forced into a life of sex slavery. They are kidnapped never to see their families and friends again."

Attorney Rossell continues her command of the meeting as she puts on her eyeglasses and reads from a note she is holding: "Naomi Schaefer Riley in her incredible book *The New Trail of Tears; The American Indians (today) have the highest rates of poverty of any racial group, (that) suicide is the leading cause of death among American Indian men, (that) American Indian women are two and a half times more likely to be raped than the national average and (that) gang violence affects American Indian youth more than any other group."*

"There is strong reason for their vulnerability. They go without what most of the others have, they are often depressed with their situation and their family's situation and way of life. They are vulnerable to being recruited into sex slavery. They are willing to go to a party in a fancy car with a nice looking young stranger when they should know better. Next thing you know they're given alcohol or drugs, raped and taken away from their homes and families.

"A second issue that has become prevalent in the mindset of our young people: Our federal government has immigrants from every third-world country on the earth, and provides everything they can to help these immigrants live the American dream. Tens of thousands of undocumented immigrants coming into our country most often have no proof of who they are or where they're from. Yet they qualify to receive all the benefits and privileges. Our government gives them housing, food, transportation, schools, and they provide interpreters and teachers who speak their language. We send them to our colleges and universities where they continue to offer courses in their languages."

Attorney Acres speaks from the podium, "Mrs. Rossell ..."

"Sir, just one more moment!" She turns back to the audience and continues.

"Then we have this same government create and establish an agency to represent the Native American Indian people. But when American Indian people seek privileges and help from our government, they are required to be a member of a federally recognized tribe through the Bureau of Indian Affairs. For starters they not only need significant qualifying documentation as to who they are, but they must prove they are descendants of their parents, grandparents, great grandparents going back to the year nineteen hundred or earlier, and that their descendants are American Indian. Once they're through that nearly impossible task, the government's purpose and goal of representation is to contain them, restrain them. Like if these Indians get out into the population, they'll mess it up. The net result, our government has treated Native Americans for centuries and still today, like crap! We are their third world."

"So, are these young people confused and vulnerable? Yes, they are. Thank you for allowing me to speak. And, please help me help them."

As Mrs. Rossell takes her seat, a scattered applause takes place beginning with the Mississippi Assistant State Attorney General and a few others. It's followed with a growing volume and number of participants.

Attorney Acres, attempting to regain his composure, says, "Yes, let's not forget who the victims are, and please, each of you, we ask that you help with this situation." He turns to Chief Gavin and Mayor Williams. "Mayor Williams, and Chief Gavin, if you have any further comments?"

Each one makes closing comments thanking the attendees for their efforts to be at today's meetings and again asks for their cooperation and help.

As the audience sifts through the coats and raingear and moves toward the exits, Attorney Acres works his way through the attendees to meet Attorney Mazie Rossell.

*   *   *

One hour later, Mayor Williams and City Attorney Acres are having a follow up lunch in his office to discuss the ten o'clock meeting.

"Hell, Mark, she just took over the meeting."

"Yeah, when I caught up with her right after the meeting I had to wait 'til she visited with three other people, including Megan Duncan, t

he Assistant State Attorney General ... she ... Rossell, wasn't the least bit apologetic. Her comment to me was, "I said what I came here to say, and I'll keep saying it until people listen and hear it. These women have rights!"

"She'll be tough to deal with, Mark. I think you and I need to be sure to keep her on our side or at least keep her in front of us. I think if we make her apart of us she can be a big help."

"Well, Mike, from what I saw and heard she has the ear of Assistant Attorney General Duncan."

"Any feedback from the other people who attended?" the mayor asks.

"No, but I will hear from one, perhaps several. No doubt in my mind we'll both get feedback. I'll keep you apprised."

Six

A critical aspect of preparation for this type of mission is to witness the pattern and habits of the offenders and criminals. Alex learned through significant stalking, that the center fourth floor casino complex parking garage of Harrah's is the usual area of the casino complex where Rick Cassel parks his white Lincoln Navigator when delivering women to the complex. Tonight he will likely leave one or more young women off at the second floor entrance where they will be met by his partner, and be delivered to men staying at the hotel who have pre-paid for sexual services. Cassel's partner, the second man, will carry the identification of the two women plus a room key for each of the hotel customers.

Given their pattern of behavior, in ninety minutes Cassel's partner will call to have Cassel meet him and the young women at the fourth floor parking garage casino entrance doors. The four will then travel to a nearby second casino hotel for the same purpose and routine. During the waiting time, Cassel will confirm their next appointments and collect credit card pre-payments.

Tonight Alex is waiting in the same center fourth floor parking garage. She's mesmerized by the familiar sounds and annoying odors of gasoline and diesel engine exhaust, along with the thumps from vehicles driving over parking garage speed bumps and parking garage expansion joints. "It's like the nuisance of a loud clock in a smoke-filled room," she whispers to herself. Her time is filled with the sounds of closing vehicle doors, their horns beeping signaling the setting of their alarms, the chatter of casino and hotel patrons anxiously arriving bringing their sounds of excitement, and their dejected silence when leaving the facility.

While waiting Alex reminds herself, "This mission is my most difficult physically and emotionally. I've designed it to punish the men and women who carry out these unpunished crimes, and bring light of the matter to everyone. In the past four days I have successfully completed my work on the first two 'nests.' Tonight will be the third. It will require every ounce of my skills, my physical and emotional strengths and instincts. My intense hatred has been set aside, not to interfere with my focus, intensity and detail. My execution must be perfect."

Twenty minutes following her arrival, she sits up straight in the driver's seat when she sees a white Lincoln Navigator pass behind her car. The driver of the Lincoln, Rick Cassel, appears to be alone. Alex instinctively crouches down in her car seat as he parks one lane over and four parking spaces to the right of her car.

Alex immediately exits her car and races to Cassel's driver's side door anxiously asking for help.

"Sir, sir, help! I need your help. I'm parked over there," she pleads pointing toward the opposite direction of her car.

She continues in a portrayed panic mode. "My girlfriend is drunk and sick. I need to call my boyfriend to come and help me take her home, but my phone is dead and I don't have my charger." She continues to plead, "Can I use your phone, just for a minute? I can give you the number and you can call ... Please?"

He pauses, then, "Okay, one quick call," he says as he exits his vehicle and hands her his cell phone.

Alex leans forward as though she's looking at the phone, then, almost instantly; she grips the blow-reed in her hand, lifts her head to face his, and blows a full tranquilizing powder dose directly into his face. Within seconds he's immobilized. She quickly opens the rear door of the Lincoln behind the driver's seat as Cassel's knees begin to buckle. As he begins to fall to the concrete floor, she pushes him onto the rear seat.

A young couple leaving the casino walks close to the commotion and changes their route to approach Alex and her efforts with Cassel. "Are you okay?" the young lady asks.

"Yeah, he's just drunk, the idiot can't even stand up," Alex grunts as she continues pushing him into the back seat.

"Let me help," the young man offers. "I can get in the other side and pull him."

A few tugs and pushes later, their efforts are successful.

"This guy's not just drunk, he's totally out of it," the man smirks.

Alex turns toward the couple, "Thank you so much for helping me," she offers, somewhat nervously and a bit winded. "The stupid jerk; that's the last time…"

"Miss, are you sure you'll be okay?" the young lady asks.

"Yes, I'm sure. I'm stone sober. I have a friend who will help me when we get home."

As the young couple regroups and turns to walk toward their vehicle, Alex smiles and waves. "Thanks again."

She catches her breath, looks around, and instinctively reaches into the side pocket of her backpack to find her latex gloves before stepping into the vehicle. In less than ten seconds, the engine of the Lincoln Navigator is humming, the lights are on, and Alex and Cassel are heading out of the parking garage.

"Okay Rickey, your date with the angels is forty-six miles away," Alex quips, as she adjusts her body to the driver's seat, exits the parking garage, and turns west onto Beach Boulevard.

As expected, there is no response or reply from the comatose man in the back seat.

"The third leg of my mission is well under way," she reminds herself, almost there. Alex has a slight but intense smile on her lips as she focuses on the planned travel west. Her mind drifts back to the preparation for this mission. It's been nearly four months of focused preparation and so far nearly perfect execution.

*   *   *

Alex arrives at a predetermined location in the Gulf Coast town of Bay St. Louis and proceeds to go to work strapping the arms and legs of her captured prey. It will be another hour before it's safe to complete strapping Cassel to the angel tree at the marina on South Beach Boulevard.

*   *   *

The forty-six mile drive back to Biloxi seems like an instant as Alex's mind drifts back to all of the training and work that has led up to this point in her life. She recalled someone telling her a person needs to spend ten thousand hours focusing and working in a career before becoming an expert. If that is so then she is surely an expert at her calling. Shaking the thought away, she reminds herself to not lose her focus by being over-confident. That would be catastrophic.

*　　*　　*

Step three of the mission is complete when I arrive at a casino parking area one-quarter mile from the casino where I abducted Cassel. Here, I abandon the Lincoln Navigator and then walk to the casino and hotel parking garage where I abducted him. The planned route takes me to the casino main entrance, then through the casino to the elevator to the fourth floor of the parking garage where I retrieve my car. Twenty-five minutes later I'm in my Ocean Springs house for a few hours rest before waking for the local morning news. I hope they've found and rescued the girls from this third 'nest.' That is the real success.

Seven

Two Bay St. Louis police officers, an early morning jogger, and the two fishermen, who discovered the body of a man tied to the 'angel tree,' are gathered near the tree adjacent to the Bay St. Louis Marina. They are awaiting the local Emergency Management Services and Bay St. Louis Police Detective, Mike Fenlon.

A third police officer arrives, exits his vehicle, and approaches the scene. "Is he alive?"

One of the police officers on the scene replies, "If he is, he's just barely. We'll know when the paramedics get here."

Bay St. Louis Police Detective Mike Fenlon arrives immediately followed by the paramedics with lights and sirens flashing and blaring. Detective Fenlon yells over the noise to identify himself then joins the paramedics tending the body. "Guys, let me take a few photos before you move him. Is he alive?"

"Man, its close Detective," replies one of the paramedics. "We need to get him on oxygen in the ambulance."

One of the Bay St. Louis police officers steps forward to help Detective Fenlon as he takes numerous photographs.

"I need a couple more photos of the bindings and the way he's tied up then take him away." He shakes his head as he sets the camera down. "I think this is similar to what they found in Biloxi."

Detective Fenlon follows the paramedics to the ambulance. "Where are you taking him?"

"To Slidell Hospital ER, it's the closest and quickest," one of the paramedics responds loudly he climbs into the back of the ambulance with the comatose man.

"Okay, I'll contact the Slidell Police and have them meet you," Detective Fenlon advises, yelling over the blaring of the sirens.

Ambulance emergency lights and more deafening sirens glare and fill the air.

*   *   *

Ten minutes later, Bay St. Louis Police Chief Gene Doyle arrives. "Is the man dead?" Chief Doyle asks one of the police officers as he walks briskly to the scene.

"The paramedics said he was still alive, Chief ... Just barely alive," replies the officer.

"Sounds like one of the pimp and prostitute situations in Biloxi," Chief Doyle mutters.

Detective Fenlon approaches Chief Doyle with a small piece of paper in his hand. "Chief, we found this note tucked into the elastic of the man's underwear."

Chief Doyle looks at the note and asks Detective Fenlon, "Is this here in Bay St. Louis. I don't recognize the address. Where the hell is it?"

"We've figured it's in Biloxi."

"So Fenlon, why in the hell is the man tied to a tree here?" Chief Doyle asks in a loud raspy voice.

Detective Fenlon looks around the scene then replies. "Damned if I know, Chief. All I know is that we'd better call Biloxi."

"Yeah, I know Chief Gavin pretty well. Fenlon, go ahead and call Biloxi P.D. Get a message to them regarding the situation here. See if they'll have Chief Gavin give me a call," commands Chief Doyle as he rubs the stubble of his beard.

Detective Fenlon retrieves the phone number from one of the other police officers and proceeds to call the Biloxi Police Department headquarters.

"Biloxi Police Department, how can I help you?"

Detective Fenlon hands the phone to Chief Doyle. "This is Chief Doyle, Bay St. Louis Police Department. We've got an emergency situation that involves a man tied to a tree with a note stuck in his underwear elastic. The note has an address of a house or business in Biloxi. It looks like the same thing you have been dealing with."

"Yes, sir, it does sound very similar."

Chief Doyle continues. "I'd like to talk to Chief Gavin as soon as possible."

"It's Chief Doyle from Bay St. Louis, correct?" asks the Biloxi police department operator.

"Yes,"

The Biloxi police operator continues. "Chief, can you give me the address you're talking about?"

"Oh yeah, let me see ..." as he squints to read the note. "It's 2631 Gordon Street. It doesn't say Biloxi."

The police operator responds. "Give me a minute. I'll check."

"Okay, Chief, yes, it looks like it's a Biloxi address. I'll get hold of Chief Gavin right away and have him call you."

"Have him call me on the number on this cell phone," Chief Gavin commands.

"Yes, sir."

*　　*　　*

Moments later, "Chief Doyle, it's Chief Gavin. I got your message. It sounds urgent."

"Chief, we found a man, near dead, half-naked, and tied to a tree at the marina in Bay St. Louis with a note stuck in his underwear elastic. The note has an address...we think it's in Biloxi."

"My operator said you had given us an address. We're checking it out. I'll call you back as soon."

"I look forward to the call, Chief," Chief Doyle says as he walks over to Detective Fenlon.

Biloxi Police Chief Gavin immediately calls his detective, Ronnie James, to advise him of the matter. Following a brief discussion, Chief Gavin contacts the head of the Biloxi SWAT team.

*　　*　　*

A television newscaster's voice excitedly announces, "Good morning and welcome to seven o'clock news from the Gulf Coast. I'm Harold Cunningham."

A second newscaster follows. "And I'm Marcie Vincent, and we're here with breaking news."

Newscaster Cunningham continues as the television screen is alive with live streaming audio and video of sirens and flashing red and white lights coming from ambulance, police and fire-rescue vehicles. Men and women wearing rescue, firefighting, and police uniforms are scurrying throughout the vehicles. "We're live at the Bay St. Louis Marina on South Beach Boulevard where the body of a man was found earlier this morning. The body was discovered at approximately five-thirty by two fishermen. According to witnesses, the partly clothed body was tied to what is known as the 'faceless angel tree.' This landmark tree died as a result of a hurricane and now has faceless angels carved into its trunk and large gray branches."

Newscaster Vincent anxiously continues the story. "We have a reporter at the site, but his system is apparently experiencing technical difficulties. What we're seeing of the scene is being filmed by our second photographer. It appears that this incident is very similar to one in Biloxi three nights ago and perhaps a second incident in Biloxi two nights ago. We'll leave this story for now and go on with the other morning news. We will break back with this story once our on-the-scene reporter is available."

*   *   *

Alex is watching the local headline news regarding the incident in Bay St. Louis. Shaking her head 'no' she stands, glares at the television and speaks loudly, "Dead, I don't think so. Not from the dose and formula I hit him with. Comatose ... in a stupor ... disabled ... no doubt...Maybe something else could have killed him. Maybe the cold weather, but I don't think so. We want him to be alive, to suffer for years and years, unable to function or communicate. These guys need to be seen in agony for years, to be in a horrible state for people to see and remember what can happen to them for committing these horrible unforgivable acts against these girls."

She turns the television set off and finishes getting ready for a long run. She is anxious to get out for a run in the cold dry morning air. She wanted to shake the news out of her head, planning a route across the bridge connecting Ocean Springs and Biloxi, then along the Biloxi beach walkway.

As she begins her run, Alex checks her watch then internalizes her plan. She would be back for the eight o'clock news and hoped by then the girls would have been found.

*   *   *

Chief Gavin receives a call from Lieutenant Bunning, team leader of the Biloxi Police Department SWAT team advising him of the successful assault on the house in question. They discovered two men and seven young women. All nine are in custody, en route to police headquarters and facilities.

At seven thirty-six a.m., a conference call from Chief Gavin to Bay St. Louis Police Chief Doyle and Detective Fenlon is underway with Chief Gavin, Detective James and Lieutenant Bunning on the Biloxi Police Department side of the call.

Following introductions, Chief Gavin is first to speak. "Chief Doyle and Detective Fenlon, let me bring you up to speed. The man's still alive. The police officer has his wallet with identification. His name is Richard Cassell and he has a New Orleans address. Apparently he's speaking gibberish, yelling and screaming, but not communicating ... much like the first two we found."

"The first two are still not able to speak," Detective James interjects.

Chief Gavin continues. "Okay, once again, our SWAT team performed their assault on the house and discovered seven women and two men. One man was shot by one of our SWAT officers while trying to escape. They are all in police custody, one on his way to the hospital, the others on their way to our police facilities. Detective James, go ahead."

"I've been assigned to lead the investigation on this case along with my involvement in the first two incidents. I'll need to work with you, Detective Fenlon, to put the Bay St. Louis incident together. It is most likely the same 'M.O.' and most likely the same people captured the guy and strapped him to the tree. It's critical we get the straps they used to tie him up and strap him to the tree plus photos taken of the man and the scene."

Detective Fenlon quickly replies. "We took dozens of photos of the man and the scene before he was removed. I can have them sent to you right away."

"Another thing, can you get to Slidell and check him out and make sure the police there are monitoring him?" Detective James requests, "I'm buried here...and be sure you have them save me the straps ... all the parts of the straps."

Chief Doyle responds, "Detective Fenlon and I will both go right after this call."

"Be sure to pick up the leather straps ... all of them, and keep them exactly the way they are. It's critical evidence." Detective James reminds them.

*   *   *

Biloxi Mayor Williams requests that Chief Gavin provide an update on what he has just witnessed on the news. Chief Gavin has hurriedly arranged a gathering of Detective James and Lieutenant Bunning to make the call to the mayor from his office.

Chief Gavin begins the call announcing he is on the speakerphone with Detective James and SWAT Team Leader Bunning in the office with him.

Mayor Williams responds. "Mark Acres is here with me. We appreciate the call. Chief, what the hell is going on?"

"Well, Mayor Williams, I got an early morning call from Police Chief Doyle that a man was bound to a tree in Bay St. Louis, with his head facing upward toward the faceless angels carved into the branches. He was barely alive. The man had a note on him with the address of a house in Biloxi. We ordered our SWAT team to the house and discovered two men and seven young women. All nine of them are in Biloxi Police custody. One man in the house attempted to escape and was shot and wounded by a SWAT team member. He is at the Biloxi hospital under police guard. The man found tied to the tree was taken to the hospital in Slidell."

Attorney Acres asks, "Chief, do we know why the man was tied to the tree in Bay St. Louis when the house is in Biloxi?"

Chief Gavin responds again. "We don't know Mark. Detective James hasn't had a chance to question or interrogate the two men found to see what they know and what they'll tell us."

"The news stated the man bound to the tree was dead," the mayor queries.

Detective James replies. "We just got off the phone with the Bay St. Louis Police Chief and their lead detective who said the man was alive, and under police guard at the Slidell hospital. Apparently, he's speaking gibberish and screaming. The two of them, the police chief and detective, are on their way to see for themselves then report back to me."

Mayor Williams takes a deep breath while drumming his fingers. He speaks. "Alright, so this man, this incident, is number three. How do we explain what's going on and why? Why all of a sudden we're discovering these young women, these sex slaves. We're being directed to find them by some person or persons capturing the men, doing something to them to put them in a stupor, and giving us directions to houses in Biloxi housing these women and their pimps. This is clearly prostitution, sex trafficking, going on here in Biloxi and we didn't know about it before this? Somebody knew about it and they're throwing it in our face."

Attorney Acres follows the mayor's words speaking in an authoritative, controlled tone. "I believe we've hit a crisis point. I suggest we gather all the information we can and get together at the mayor's office conference room...it's a little after eight now, let's say eleven o'clock. That gives us more than two hours to put together some response for the chamber of commerce, FBI, the press and all the others."

"Eleven o'clock it is," says the mayor thumping his fingers on his desk.

Each of the three in Chief Gavin's office mumbles his agreement.

The conference call concludes. Detective James looks at Chief Gavin and Lieutenant Bunning and says, "Whoever is capturing and putting these guys on display has either really done his or their homework or they're a part of this whole thing. They know who they are and what they're doing. Unfortunately, gentlemen, we don't. I think we … us … we are in for one hell of a beating from the mayor and everyone else."

*   *   *

At the conclusion of the conference call, Mayor Williams and the city attorney agree to schedule a closed meeting at the city council chambers at two o'clock this afternoon. It will be followed by an open meeting press conference. Those invited to attend the closed meeting include Mayor Williams, City Attorney Acres, Chairman of the Biloxi City Council, President of the Biloxi Chamber of Commerce, two casino security chiefs, Biloxi Chief of Police Gavin, Detective James, Lieutenant Bunning, the County Prosecuting Attorney John Darlson, Lawrence Gustafson, a Special Agent with the Federal Bureau of Investigation assigned to the case, Senior Agent Jeffrey Cooper of the Mississippi Bureau of Investigation, Carl Jason, a representative of the Bureau of Indian Affairs, and Megan Duncan, the Mississippi Assistant State Attorney General.

*   *   *

Alex returns from her run somewhat refreshed and is glued to her television screen awaiting the eight o'clock news.

The wide-screen television screen flashes 'URGENT UPDATE' accompanied by the audio spurting a dynamic theme.

An exuberant newscaster begins, "Good morning and welcome to an urgent update and our eight o'clock news live from the Gulf Coast. I'm Harold Cunningham." The second newscaster follows."And, I'm Marcie Vincent, and we're here with breaking news." She continues as scenes shown on their seven o'clock report repeat. "We're here with an important update on the early morning news bulletin."

Newscaster Cunningham returns. "We have received new information on the status of the man found early this morning tied to the angel tree at the Bay St. Louis Marina. The man is reported to be alive but in critical condition. The Bay St. Louis Police made the announcement just minutes ago."

The cameras move back to Newscaster Vincent who continues. "The incident is believed to be related to two recent incidents in Biloxi where men were found, partially clothed, either tied to a tree or in the back of a pickup truck. Each of these two previous incidents led to the discovery of young women being used as sex slaves; forced into sex slavery. We will keep you informed of any further breaking news regarding this story."

"Now to other eight o'clock news,"

Alex, standing in her jogging clothing, performs a fist pump. "Excellent!" she blurts out. "Take my shower, meditate, then I'm ready for a full day of preparation for the last leg of the mission. Still much to do," she reminds herself.

Eight

Attorney Mazie Rossell grips the steel handrail at the foot of the four concrete steps leading up to the Biloxi Medical Center. The cold, wet weather continues its hold on the Biloxi area making stairways such as this close to icy. Two elderly women waiting for the doors to open for the day's business follow Mrs. Rossell using the same caution. Once inside the center Attorney Rossell quickly approaches the receptionist's window to announce her intentions.

A nervous receptionist asks, "May I help you?"

"Yes, I'm Attorney Rossell. I'm here to meet with the seven women who were brought into police custody this morning."

The receptionist replies nervously. "I think you need to speak to the police officers. Let me get one of them," she says as she turns to a co-worker.

The receptionist watches Attorney Rossell pace a dozen steps back and forth in the waiting area. The two elderly women who followed Mrs. Rossell into the building are sitting together in the waiting area, each dressed in their winter coat, each clutching their purse held in their lap. Both women follow the pacing intently. Four minutes pass as she continues to widen the area of her pacing; now throughout the entire waiting area.

A police woman in full police uniform, minus the hat, walks into the waiting area, approaches Attorney Rossell, offers her hand for an introductory handshake and, with a firm smile, introduces herself, "Attorney Rossell, I'm Lieutenant Carol Rose. How can I help you?"

"I'm pleased to meet you Lieutenant Rose," she replies with a firm handshake.

"Lieutenant, I represent several of the young women who have been placed in Biloxi Police custody as a result of the discovery of the sex trafficking incidents."

Lieutenant Rose focuses her attention on Attorney Rossell. "Yes, it's a tragic situation. I'm so thankful they've been found. And, yes, I'm aware that you represent several of the women. However, none of the young women in our custody have been charged with any wrongdoing or crimes. We are still in the processing stage."

Mazie Rossell continues. "Lieutenant, I'm here to introduce myself to the new women found last night... the seven new ones discovered earlier this morning. I'm here to offer my services as an attorney for several reasons. Each of these young victims should be represented by an attorney in case they have any charges brought against them; each one has a right to an attorney when they are being questioned about the incidents and wrongdoings of the men. They are entitled to be represented by an attorney to discuss the likelihood of being called as a witness against their captors for rape, kidnapping, and bringing them here across state lines then selling each of them into prostitution and sex slavery. A number of these women are American Indians ... Native Americans, and the American Indian people have a long history of being mistreated and misrepresented by government agencies and police."

Lieutenant Rose looks straight at Attorney Rossell and replies. "Yes, they are in our custody. With all due respect, ma'am, the seven just arrived here within the hour. You'll have to discuss your request with the public defender's office and the prosecuting attorney's office, see where they are in their process and, I believe, advise them of your intentions. In the meantime, I'll advise them and our police headquarters of your request and that you are here."

"Thank you Lieutenant. I'll start with the public defenders," as she quickly turns to exit the building she grips the cold, wet handrail then walks gingerly to her car.

It is eleven o'clock in the morning; Mayor Williams, City Attorney Mark Acres, and Police Chief Gavin are meeting in the mayor's office. Attorney Acres announces to the other two, "I have to make a quick call to the County Prosecuting Attorney, John Darlson. I'd like for the two of you to listen in on the speaker phone."

Both agree.

"John, this is Mark Acres calling to follow up on our conversation an hour-or-so ago."

"Yes sir, Mark, go ahead."

"John, we're discussing the handling of each of the young women in our care or custody. First, I suggest we consider them to be in our care, not custody."

"I agree," said the prosecuting attorney.

"Next, John, I believe it's best to remind each of them that they are not being charged with anything at this time, that each of them receives their full Miranda rights regarding their rights to an attorney, that your office will provide them with an attorney at no cost to them if they feel they need one. I suggest you advise each of them that they are being held for medical and emotional treatment and their safety, and that we will do everything we can to help them contact their parents, friends and families."

"Mr. Acres, I agree with your suggestions. We've done all of those things with each of the young women we have in custody...well, we'll finish today with the new women found last night. My question is, how long can we keep them in custody or our care? How long do we keep them here? Where do we put them, and the state prosecutors want to know about needing witnesses against their procurers?"

"John, we're discussing that as we speak. Our challenge is to come up with a plan so that all of the Biloxi, the Mississippi, and the federal prosecutors are properly included. Right now, today, we all need to be sure they're given their rights and assurance they're being kept safe and we're providing for them."

John pauses then speaks. "One more question. What about the lady attorney, Mrs. Rossell? She has already been to my office this morning. She expects a call from me as soon as possible."

"Good question, John. It has to be handled correctly. The girls have a right to their own attorney, but this will be discussed during this afternoon's meeting along with a number of other issues. I'll call you as soon as we finish our meeting."

"Thanks, Mark, and thanks Mayor Williams and Chief Gavin. Sorry to have taken so much of your time."

Mayor Williams leans over the speaker. "Be sure to call me directly any time, and we'll see you at the two o'clock meeting."

As the three regroup following the call, Mayor Williams turns to Chief Gavin while rapidly tapping his fingers on his desk. "So, Chief, where in hell are we with this fiasco?"

"I'm not aware of any two o'clock meeting. That's today?" asks Chief Gavin. "I must have missed something."

"Actually, Chief, Mark and I called the meeting. Sorry we hadn't notified you earlier," replies the mayor.

"Chief, you're here now to help us prepare for the two o'clock," advises Attorney Acres.

"Let me get back to your question Mike." Chief Gavin turns in his chair to face Mayor Williams and draws his hands together while leaning back. "Okay, let me start with today. I received a call from Chief Doyle, Bay St. Louis. He advised me that they had a man, nearly or possibly dead, tied to the faceless angel tree at the marina. Same story, stripped down to his underwear with a note in his underwear elastic with an address they believed was here in Biloxi. Paramedics took him to the emergency hospital in Slidell."

Attorney Acres abruptly interrupts. "Slidell is in Louisiana. We need to get him back here, in Mississippi. Why in hell did they take him there?"

Chief Gavin replies, "Sir, I wasn't there, but my guess is that Slidell is closer or faster to get to than Biloxi."

Mayor Williams speaks. "That's probably correct. Chief, please continue."

"We sent Lieutenant Bunning and his SWAT team to the address. Sure enough, they found seven more young women plus two other men. The seven young women are in custody...or our care at the medical center. The other men arrested at the house are being questioned under suspicion of sex trafficking and dealing with prostitution. One of the two men was shot by a member of the SWAT team. He's in police custody at the hospital, not seriously injured. They're questioning him there."

Mayor Williams stands up from his seat, rubs the back of his neck then speaks. "What we have here is a nightmare!"

Attorney Acres follows as he stands up from his chair and begins to pace around the mayor's office. He begins to speak as he looks at the floor."Gentlemen, we got together to discuss how to address the group at the two o'clock. We have a few hours to put together an agenda for that meeting so that it doesn't become a free-for-all."

Attorney Acres and Mayor Williams continue to pace around the office in silence. Attorney Acres breaks the silence. "Let's start with the facts. We have a situation here in Biloxi that could be the greatest catastrophe since Hurricane Katrina. We have eleven young women, one as young as fourteen, being used as prostitutes. We found another seven today, so we have eighteen total. Then we believe two more might be, or are missing; that makes twenty! We have three men in a stupor or dead, found tied to trees or in the back end of a pickup truck put there by somebody. Then we have four other men who we believe are...I guess we are calling them procurers, who are in jail under suspicion of procurement for prostitution, sex trafficking of young women as young as fourteen, sex trafficking across state lines; interstate sex trafficking. Then we discover several of these young women are Native American. That's just for starters."

Mayor Williams sits heavily into his chair, and looks at the two men. "Mark, Chief, do we have any suspects for the person out there who has captured the men responsible for running these prostitution groups? Who has captured, drugged or terrorized them into a stupor before putting them on public display?"

Chief Gavin sinks into his chair and once again draws his hands together in front of himself. "No sir, we don't have anybody by name. Detective James has produced a few ideas for profiles, but no specific suspects. But this morning we put out an emergency all-points bulletin to all Biloxi police officers. The county did the same with all the sheriff's personnel. We also advised all of the heads of hotel security. We have three detectives assigned to head up a manhunt operation to find whoever is capturing the pimps. We also believe the ones we've captured, the ones who are still coherent, know something so we're questioning them real hard."

Attorney Acres speaks as he is walking away from Chief Gavin. "You realize, Chief, the two o'clock meeting is going to be a rough one for you...actually for all of us. But there are a lot of fingers being pointed at you and your officers for not knowing about the prostitution here."

"Yes sir," the chief replies. "But let me finish. When we do find the ones capturing the pimps, we'll be able to learn if there are any more, and who and where they are."

The mayor speaks while slowly shaking his head and nervously drumming his fingers on the corner of his desk. "Chief, the point is how does someone else know so much about the prostitution activities and you and your officers don't? That's the question you'll be confronted with at two o'clock."

Attorney Acres looks at the other two. "I think we need to take the rest of the time we have and get prepared with an agenda and plans for the two o'clock meeting. I'm guessing Attorney Rossell will be there along with all the rest, including state and federal people and the media."

Nine

The high pressure weather system over southern Mississippi and Louisiana brings the relief of clear skies and sunshine. The cool dry day provides a welcome relief to the damp musty odor from the hats, coats and sweaters in the room compared to the past two meetings. The city council chamber was once again packed with anxious invited parties. The bubbling solemn and rumor-filled chatter is present throughout the room.

Attorney Mazie Rossell is seated at the end left seat, third row back facing the podium. Attorney Acres' twelve-thirty call to invite her was followed by an early entry into the council chambers to claim a key seat location; one that commands a good speaking post visible to most of the attendees; one where most can see her without turning around or looking for her lost in the audience. Her voice will be equally effective from this vantage.

City Attorney Mark Acres enters the room wearing his courtroom suit. Following a few handshakes and quick acknowledgments, he walks quickly to the podium. He glances around the room and promptly at two o'clock, without hesitation, speaks into the microphone."Welcome, once again."

He pauses momentarily to allow the chatter to stop, then, "Our goal today is once again to bring you up to date with the difficult situation involving sex trafficking and prostitution in Biloxi and the surrounding area. We have with us a number of state, local, and federal officials and representatives of officials who have agreed to assist and pledge their agencies assistance in helping resolve this issue."

"First, we'll provide details of a third incident, this one involving a man bound and nearly dead found in Bay St. Louis early this morning. A note found on the man directed us to a third house in Biloxi where more young women were found. Next, we will bring you up to date regarding the persons and young women found in the first two instances, and third, we'll detail a plan of action that is being implemented as-we-speak to deal with all of this."

Attorney Acres glances quickly at Mayor Williams and Police Chief Gavin both seated to his left.

"This third incident took place in Bay St. Louis early this morning with a call to the Bay St. Louis police that a person or body had been discovered with hands and legs bound in a matter much like the first two incidents. This time his head was fixed so his face was aimed at the faceless angels carved into the branches of the angel tree at the Bay St. Louis Marina. A note attached to his nearly nude body directed the Bay St. Louis and Biloxi Police to another house in Biloxi."

"This brings the total to seven men believed to be captors and purveyors of the young women. They are in the process of being charged with numerous crimes including kidnapping, rape, sex trafficking and interstate crimes of the same nature. A group, including the Harrison County Prosecuting Attorney is joined by the Mississippi Attorney General's Office and federal attorneys to draft these charges. Their work is hampered by the fact that three of the men captured or found, remain totally incoherent from the infliction of some sort of drug or substance, unknown to us at this time, inflicted by the person or persons who captured them, bound them, and placed them on public display to be found."

He pauses, and continues. "The eighteen young women found, eleven from the two previous incidents plus seven from the third incident, are being treated and cared for by Biloxi and county doctors and nurses along with other health care and mental health personnel. We have requested additional health and mental health care professionals from other counties and the State of Mississippi. I'd like to introduce one of the key members of these health care professionals, Doctor Rachel Larsen from the local Harrison County Office of the Mississippi State Health Department, to provide us with an update. Doctor Larsen."

"Yes, Mr. Acres. Let me start with the statistics, the status of the eighteen women including those discovered last night or this morning. We and the police officials believe there are two more young women not yet found. Ten of those found are believed to be Native American or American Indian from three different states, including Mississippi. Two of the young women are of Asian descent, three are Caucasian, one Hispanic and two are mixed-race. We believe they are between fifteen and twenty-one years of age. Our work with them includes mental therapy, physical therapy, medical treatment and two are in serious need of dental treatment. Folks, we have our hands full."

Doctor Larsen looks up from her notes and continues.

"We all need to put ourselves in their shoes. I'll summarize what we have heard from a few of the young women. 'You're a fifteen or sixteen year old Native American girl living in a rural area, perhaps a small community or town, maybe on an Indian reservation. You likely have brothers or sisters, maybe both. You likely live at a subsistence level. Hopefully, each one has a mother and father living in the same house, perhaps a grandparent. You have aunts and uncles, cousins living next door or nearby. That's your comfort."

She pauses, "That's your home. You likely have a pet, dog or cat, perhaps farm animals you care for and feed. Each pet and farm animal has a name. They too are part of your family, your comfort. Your school is most likely run-down, poorly equipped with questionable heat and no air conditioning for the hot days. Your teacher or teachers are poorly paid; perhaps working there for the experience or out of the goodness of their hearts. Nevertheless, they are your teachers, part of your comfort ... your world."

She pauses again, clears her throat. "Now you wake up one morning and you're not at your home. What you have is suddenly gone. Your body hurts, your head hurts, your eyes aren't seeing well, you rub them and take time to focus. You look around; don't know where you are. Your mother, father, aunts, uncles, grandparents, sisters, brothers, cousins, best friends, boyfriends, girlfriends, teachers, church pastor, church friends, your books, your clothes, all of your possessions, everything in your life is gone. Your family pet, even your farm animals you help feed before going to school ...gone. A man you vaguely recognize opens the door to your room with nothing but a single bed. You break into uncontrollable tears realizing you're going to be raped again.' "

The room was absolutely silent. She continues, "We must all realize what a tragedy this is for these beautiful young women. These are not events or incidents. They are human tragedies. Yes, we have our hands full. We need all the help you can give."

"Let me finish with this. Treatments for the first two groups of women are scheduled and underway. Our goal is to complete scheduling of all treatments by the end of our work-day tomorrow. All eighteen women are or will be housed at an undisclosed, secured facility with twenty-four-seven health care available. Their wellbeing is our primary goal. We are working with them understanding their recovery is long term and that they will suffer the difficulty of being able and available to serve as witnesses in the prosecution of the men and women who kidnapped, raped, and sold them into sex slavery." Doctor Larsen nods then walks back to her seat.

A quiet hush fills the room as Mark Acres quickly moves back to the podium.

"Doctor Larsen, thank you so much. They are also being represented and counseled by a group of legal professionals including one we recognize being here today, Attorney Mazie Rossell. Mrs. Rossell, please stand."

Attorney Rossell stands quickly and briefly while thanking Attorney Acres and Doctor Larsen for her outstanding presentation. Attorney Acres continues, "Attorney Rossell represents each of the ten young women believed to be Native American, and has offered her services to the other eight. Folks, We all have a most difficult task going forward. One of the complexities will be the likelihood of interstate sex trafficking and kidnapping. It will likely involve these young victims being required to testify, or at least help build the cases against their captors. The total numbers of captors and young victims will require massive hours of work and rehabilitation."

As Attorney Acres pauses for a drink of water, a male attendee shouts out from the audience: "Maybe you need to hire the statistician from the Biloxi Shuckers Baseball team to help keep track."

Several members of the audience raise their voices denouncing the man and his comments.

"Sir, that's not appropriate, in fact, distasteful," shouts Mayor Williams as he stands and faces the man.

Attorney Acres shuffles the papers in front of him. "Sir, that really doesn't help us." He continues, "Finally we have the task of finding who has captured the three men, bound then and placed them on display with the message of where to find the young women and their captors. At this moment we do not have any specific suspects. A task force of the Biloxi Police Department and detective force along with members of the local sheriff's offices, members of the Mississippi Bureau of Investigation, the Mississippi State Police and the Federal Bureau of Investigation are working the dual role of finding this person or these persons, and working with the prosecuting attorneys to develop charges against the captors of the women. I'll ask Biloxi Detective Ronnie James to address this."

A news reporter stands and speaks loudly. "Can we ask questions? Why haven't the Biloxi Police known about these prostitutes and this activity?"

"We'll have time for a few questions when Detective James is through with his comments," notes Attorney Acres as he nods to the reporter and invites Detective James to the podium.

Detective James moves slowly to the podium. His demeanor and appearance give signs of his exhausting week. He slowly looks at the audience with a tired stare and speaks. "Today Mayor Williams and Police Chief Gavin asked FBI Special Agent, Lawrence Gustafson and me to put together a team specifically focused on finding the person or persons who have captured and displayed the three comatose men. Our combined efforts based on a number of factors tell us there are two or more, likely male, likely physically strong, likely Native American, and most likely highly trained individuals for this type of activity. There is very little history of this type of activity known to federal or state law enforcement."

Following two drinks of water, Detective James continues. "We are meeting immediately after this session with a number of hotel and casino security personnel, county and local police and sheriff's representatives to discuss our suspicions and provide a list of things and activities to look for while considering suspects. Second, we have asked our police and local sheriff's officers to search every possible hint of prostitution in Biloxi and neighboring cities and towns. This is the equivalent of a significant 'man-hunt' for both prostitution activities and the suspected Native Americans who have put the three in comatose condition then on display. That's all I have for now."

Attorney Acres quickly moves to the podium and microphone amid loud requests to ask questions. He speaks loudly over the noise. "I've been instructed by Mayor Williams to conclude this meeting so that the medical and law enforcement groups and personnel can get to their meetings can get on with their work."

"Thanks for being here," he yells out to the crowd as he, Chief Gavin and Mayor Williams move quickly toward the side door.

Detective James moves quickly through the exiting crowd to introduce himself to Attorney Rossell and Doctor Larsen who are engaged in conversation.

Following his introduction to the two he turns to find Federal Bureau Agent Gustafson engaged in conversation with Mississippi Bureau Senior Agent Cooper. Agent Gustafson motions for Detective James to join them.

"Ronnie, I think Agent Cooper has something we should look at, "says Agent Gustafson intently.

He continues. "Agent Cooper has an idea we need to endorse. Go ahead … share your idea with Ronnie."

"I think there's more to this Indian thing than we know at this point. I have an uncle who is a Choctaw Indian elder… lives in the sticks in Mississippi. I'm going to meet with him tomorrow. It's a couple of hours from here, but I think it might be worth the trip."

"Could be a long shot, but I like the idea," Detective James noted.

"I believe we need to look more closely at what the Indian involvement is … there's something here, not just the young women and Attorney Rossell. I'm beginning to feel it."

Agent Gustafson says as he looks around the empty chambers room. "I like the idea … I like it a lot. If your gut is urging you to go, then you should go."

"Be sure to ask about the square knots," Detective James reminds him as he signals it's time to go and walks toward the exit door.

Ten

It's nine fourteen p.m. at Treasure Bay Casino. Flashing lights and deafening sirens from Biloxi police vehicles are joined by flashing lights of an ambulance and a Harrison County police car lit up the casino's covered canopy entrance. More than a dozen police officers and sheriff's deputies have mobbed the entrance. News reporters are clamoring to get close to the center of the action to record the commotion and get photos. Casino patrons and other spectators have joined the commotion, rapidly accelerating into bedlam. Two Biloxi police motorcycle officers are loudly working their way to the front of the entrance to lead the caravan of police vehicles from the Treasure Bay Casino scene to police headquarters.

At the casino entrance doorway, the center of the commotion, two men are lying face down with hands handcuffed behind their backs.

Biloxi Police Lieutenant Bunning is screaming orders with his hands cupped around his mouth in his attempt to create a megaphone effect. His voice is drowned by police sirens, engines of a dozen cars, police motorcycles and other police vehicles, plus the yelling and screaming of numerous other police officers and a few dozen onlookers.

"Alright, listen-up. Harold, you and Pechta get these two men off the ground and into the two police cars, one in each car. Stay right behind the two motorcycle officers. They'll escort you. You know the rule; don't let anybody get between you and the motorcycles. Martin you get behind the second one, Becker, you get behind Martin."

The handcuffed men are pulled up from their facedown position by two police officers each, one on each upper arm, and quickly placed into the waiting police cars. Lieutenant Bunning moves quickly to the front of the two motorcycle officers leading the caravan of cars, anxiously waving his arms to indicate 'get going.' The six vehicles with the two handcuffed men leave the casino site, turn onto North Beach Boulevard and with, lights flashing and sirens screaming, head toward their police headquarters.

*   *   *

"This is Gulf Coast News at eleven o'clock. Good evening, I'm Mary McKinnon with breaking news."

"And I'm Darrell Jensen. We're bringing you our live report from outside the Biloxi Police Department Headquarters where our on-site reporter Craig Wilson is live. Craig!"

"Thanks Darrell. I'm outside the Biloxi Police Department Headquarters where we're told the two men taken into custody earlier this evening are still inside. The two men are suspects in the ongoing and complex sex trafficking case. According to police sources, they are being held for questioning as suspects in relation to the case where three men have been drugged, and then bound, two of them to a tree where they were found the next day. The men who were found had notes placed on them that led the police to houses where they discovered several young women who were being used as prostitutes. Again, the two men taken into police custody tonight are being held under suspicion of doping and doing significant harm to those three men."

"Craig, this is Mary McKinnon. I'm here with Darrell. Have the police given you any information as to when they might make an announcement or have further information available?"

"No Mary, they have not. I'm here along with a dozen or more media people. We're camped out here for the night. I'll bring you up-to-date as soon as any further information is available."

"Thanks Craig. Now, on to other news…"

*   *   *

Prosecuting Attorney Darlson and Detective Ronnie James are at the police headquarters on a phone call to Chief Gavin. It's eleven fourteen pm.

"Chief, the two men have been taken into police custody on suspicion of doing significant bodily harm to the three men," says Attorney Darlson.

"Be sure to get the names of the two bound and doped men we know. We're not sure of the name of the third man. And, be sure the charges are correct and include these two men's names." Chief Gavin advises.

Darlson replies, "Chief, we can add charges, and we can hold them on these charges for now. But before we question them we need to have one charge we'll use for sure. I've had a discussion with the state attorney general so I'm comfortable with this one. So, Chief, Detective James and I would like to begin the interrogation right away to see what we can get out of them. I plan to have myself and my assistant prosecuting attorney question one of the men while Detective James and another police officer question the other."

"Okay, you and Ronnie see each one separately first. Keep them separated, read them their rights, advise them what charges they're being held on, then go ahead with your interrogation."

Detective James asks, "Chief, one question before we disconnect. Can we impound their car or cars and search their rooms? We have their car keys and room keys here...they had to empty their pockets."

Prosecuting Attorney Darlson adds, "If we can't or don't think we can, we can put their cars and rooms under surveillance; put police officers at their room entrance and at their cars. I'd suggest we get officers over their right now to guard them."

"We can't let anybody get into the rooms or cars, clean them up or disturb any evidence," says Ronnie James.

"When we get the okay to impound them, I'd like to do that," says Darlson. "I believe they're staying at Treasure Bay. Their security chief will know."

Chief Gavin: "Okay, I'll get that taken care of, you two go ahead with the questioning. Maybe you'll learn something right away. Let me know what you find."

*   *   *

Twenty minutes later, Detective Ronnie James and Assistant Detective Jimmy Halverson along with the first detained man are seated in an interrogation room. Prosecuting Attorney Darlson and his assistant are seated in another interrogation room with the second detained man. Prior to questioning, Detective James and Prosecuting Attorney Darlson introduce themselves to the detained men, read each his Miranda Rights, and then advised them in detail, that they are being held for questioning on suspicion of doing significant bodily harm to three men on three specific occasions.

In the first room, Detective James asks the detained man, "Sir, what is your full name?"

"Lollie Shedawin," the man replies.

Detective James stares at his note pad as he asks, "Lolly; L-O-L-L-Y?"

"No, L-O-L-L-I-E. It's on my driver's license. You have my wallet and my driver's license."

"Okay sir, and where do you live."

"That's on my driver's license too. I live in Saraland, Alabama, just outside Mobile ...2782 Loblolly Lane, Saraland, Alabama. I own the house there."

"Mr. Shedawin, what do you do there? What is your occupation?"

"I'm a welder. I work in the shipyards."

"And, when did you arrive in Biloxi?"

"I came here yesterday ...yesterday around noon."

"And, Mr. Shedawin, where are you staying?"

"We're staying at Treasure Bay. Me and my brother Gordon come here twice a year...we always stay at the same place."

"Your brother, Gordon, is the other man in custody?"

"Yeah, I don't know why we're here or why we've been arrested," says Shedawin throwing his hands and arms up. "We just came here like we do every year. We didn't hurt anybody. We come here, gamble, and spend some money. Ask the hotel."

"Mr. Shedawin, did you and your brother drive here together?" Detective James asks trying to gain control of the interrogation.

"Sir, I think I need to call our lawyer. Me and my brother both use the same lawyer. He's in Mobile. I've got his number in my cell phone. So I need my cell phone."

Detective James stands then exits the room and motions to Prosecuting Attorney Darlson through the interrogation room window to step outside the room.

"John, it looks like we need to pause, or stop the questioning. This Lollie guy just lawyered up. He's calling his lawyer. He said he and his brother use the same one."

*　　*　　*

Prosecuting Attorney Darlson and Detective James are seated in a small conference room. The two detained men have been placed in a detention cell.

"Crap, Ronnie. Their attorney is on his way here from Mobile."

"John, I don't see how we can continue to detain these two. According to Treasure Bay management, they're telling the truth. They stay at the hotel like they said. They even ran a tab the last two times."

"I thought Treasure Bay security called this in," states Darlson.

Detective James replies, "I believe they did. I guess they didn't check with other Treasure Bay people first. Hell, these guys are their customers."

Attorney Darlson turns looking directly at Detective James, "Ronnie, what about their car or cars, and their room at Treasure Bay?"

"You didn't hear this from me. I'm told they are clean, both the room and the cars. We ran their driver's license and auto tags plus whatever police records we could from Alabama. They're both clean."

Prosecuting Attorney Darlson stands up from his seat, looks away from Detective James. "Okay, let's get hold of Chief Garvin ... give him the news."

*   *   *

At four twenty-five a.m., a man dressed in Levi pants and a white cotton collared shirt walks up to the man at the front desk of the police headquarters, hands the officer his business card and states, "My name is Charles Kessler. I'm here to meet with my client Lollie Shedawin."

"Sir, please have a seat. I'll have someone come out to meet you."

"Thank you officer, but I prefer to stand."

*   *   *

The television screen blasts the scene from last night's bedlam at the Treasure Bay Casino entrance with the 'BREAKING NEWS' stripe across the bottom of the screen. "This is Gulf Coast Morning News at seven o'clock. I'm Harold Cunningham,"

"And I'm Marcie Vincent. Let's get right to our breaking news story. We're bringing you our live report from Biloxi Police Headquarters where our on-site reporter Craig Wilson is live. Good morning, Craig, bring us up to date."

"Thanks, Marcie. I'm outside the Biloxi Police Department Headquarters where Prosecuting Attorney John Darlson stepped outside a few minutes ago and read a brief statement regarding the release of the two men held for questioning in the sex trafficking case. We have a recording of that statement."

The tape begins. Dozens of lights from media cameras light the early morning dimness. "I'm Prosecuting Attorney John Darlson. At six fifteen this morning the two men being held for questioning in the recent sex trafficking scandal were released without any charges being brought against them. That's all I have."

A news reporter asks, "So, there wasn't any evidence that they were involved?"

97

Attorney Darlson responds, "There wasn't sufficient evidence. Okay, that's all. Thank you all for being here."

Marcie Vincent returns to the television screen. "Craig, is there any discussion of why they arrested the two men? From all the commotion when they arrested them...I think the police were pretty rough on the two."

Reporter Craig Wilson replies. "Marcie, Yes. Among the media a lot of talk about that; there is the fact that the two men are believed to be Native American. Rumor here is that the two men have an attorney. We're all hopeful that we will hear from him."

"Interesting... Thanks Craig, now to other morning news."

Eleven

It's nine thirty in the morning. Senior Agent Cooper has been traveling for nearly two hours while fielding a barrage of cell phone calls and texts regarding last night's Treasure Bay fiasco. He's finally free of calls due to the terrible cell phone access in this area. He is traveling to meet with his uncle Mitchell Ward, a Choctaw Indian elder. At this point in his travel, he is being escorted by Mitchell's granddaughter, Nina. Agent Cooper met Nina at her home sixteen miles from their destination. Mitchell's home is located in very remote Mississippi. As they leave her home, Nina guides her uncle, Agent Cooper, onto a Mississippi State Road.

"Nina, it's been years since I've been here. Your father drove me here the last time."

"If you remember, Uncle Jeffrey, we'd better stop at the Shell station before we leave the main road. Grandpa's facilities aren't very pleasant."

Following their 'pit-stop' they turn onto a two-lane blacktop road which soon becomes a gravel road and eventually becomes a gravel and sand road with deep ditches on either side.

During the ride they pass a few dozen homes, a mix of motor homes, manufactured homes, and a few that have deteriorated into shacks.

"Nina, are the people here Indians?"

"Mostly, yes. Some are our relatives, but most of the people here have lived here for years. There's not much work around here. Most just live off their government checks, you know, retirement and disability. There's no Indian money here. Grandpa still makes stuff and sells to people he's sold to for years. Two other people here do the same and Aunt Minnie does a lot of crafts and sells to a place near where I live."

Suddenly, Nina sits up in her seat, "There, over there, see that old road," she points anxiously. "Turn there...turn onto that road... right there with the broken sign. We're almost there."

Approximately one hundred yards after turning onto the road, it becomes the semblance of an abandoned gravel and tar surface with grass and weeds growing through. As they bump along the roadway they pass remnants of an abandoned Pure Oil gas station with the sign hanging sideways at what appears to be an intersection. Two other dilapidated cement block structures are visible thru the tall weeds and trees growing inside and outside the crumbling walls.

In less than a minute another abandoned building comes into view. As the road leads them to the right a second and third building appear, again, abandoned. On the left appears a welcome sight, Uncle Mitchell's trailer. Agent Cooper turns toward it declaring, "Nina, that's it right?"

"Yes, sir, we're here," she replies excitedly.

There it stands. The 1960 Shasta Air-Flyte, one room travel trailer with perfect Tennessee orange-colored trim. "It's exactly how I remember." exclaims Cooper.

Immediately to the right of the trailer is a shed with a one piece garage door wide open. The shed displays all its handcrafted goods, tools, and in front of it all is Uncle Mitchell with a smile that covers the entire bottom of his face.

"Come in, Come in," he says motioning with his arms as he stands waiting for the car to stop.

"Hey, come on in, have a seat. Come on in to the workshop. It's cooler here. We'll get some breeze," as he shuffles to gather a third wooden chair.

The workshop is a shed with the front of the shed consisting of a small garage door. Inside several dream catchers, two with peacock feathers, hang on one side of the workshop. Hand carved wooden birds are strewn on the waist-high work bench and an assortment of carving tools and paper and other work tools lay beside the carved birds. Three archery bows under construction, with four or five layers of wood glued and held together with clamps, stand in the corner opposite the dream catchers.

"I don't get a lot of visitors, so two chairs is usually all I need," as he quickly approaches Jeffrey with a hug. "It's always good to see you, Jeffrey."

Jeffrey opens a brown paper bag and pulls out a sixty-four ounce clear plastic jar filled with assorted color and flavored jelly beans. "This is for you, Uncle Mitchell. Gladys said, 'Don't show up without it.'"

With the jar of jelly beans in one arm he reaches out to shake Jeffrey's hand. "Tell Gladys thanks. She remembered these are my favorites...see, forty-nine flavors," as he looks down at the large candy filled gift. "How is Gladys?" He asks as he sets the jar on his work bench.

"Gladys is doing great. She and the kids are all doing well," Jeffrey responded.

Nina had stepped into the conversation a few moments before the jelly bean presentation. "Grandpa, I don't need to stay for all of this, so I might just wander off in a few, leave you two alone to talk. I can always work on cleaning your trailer," she says with a sly smile.

"Sure, Nina. That's okay. You might like to just look around the old house where grandma and I used to live. And, the TV in the trailer gets two channels if you want to watch it."

Nina looks back at Grandpa Mitchell, "Grandpa, I brought sandwiches for lunch. They're in the cooler in the car. Your refrigerator is pretty small."

"Thanks, Nina. We'll let you know when."

Mitchell speaks first. "Jeff, we're all so proud of what you have become. We know how hard you worked for what you have."

Jeffrey speaks while looking around the workshop. "Uncle Mitchell, I'm always impressed when I see your work. It's remarkable. And it looks like you're doing well."

He shuffles his chair to be facing Mitchell. "When I called you about coming here to see you, I mentioned I needed to ask you for your help ... a few questions about a case I'm working on. It's different. I believe it might have to do with Indian skill and activities. It seems to be beyond what any of us in the conventional law enforcement world understand. It has the police detectives, the FBI, all of us baffled."

"Jeffrey, you can ask me anything. I'll tell you what I know or think and it is all a secret, or as you guys say 'confidential.' I won't tell anybody. Look around. It's just me, my dog Charlie and four chickens."

"Thanks," Agent Cooper replies as he crouches slightly looking directly at his uncle. "We have a situation regarding men kidnapping young women, many of them young Indian girls, taking them to a city where they sell them each day and evening as prostitutes."

Mitchell shakes his head side to side as he looks at the ground. "Man, that's bad ... that's really bad."

"The other part of this is that there is someone capturing these evil men and doping them into a stupor, tying them to trees where the public will find them. Then they place feathers on them and notes directing them to where they can find these victimized young women."

"I'm listening, Jeffrey," Mitchell says as he squints at Jeffrey.

"Okay, let me continue. One of the clues we have is that the men strapped to the trees are bound with three-eighth inch soft leather straps. Each one is identical and every knot is an identical perfect square knot...identical."

As Agent Cooper pauses, Mitchell clears his throat and raises his right hand with his first two fingers pointed upward. "I can help you there. Two types of Indians tie perfect square knots. One is women. The second is craftsmen, either man or woman. Let me show you. I tie square knots all the time with my work. Like the square knots in my dream catchers."

Mitchell retrieves two pieces of quarter-inch leather strands from his work bench and holds them in his hands in front of Jeffrey. "Okay. To tie the knot, hold the twine or strap with your first two fingers and thumb with each hand. Go left–over-right then snug the straps to the tightness you want. They should never be too tight. It messes up the knot. Now, hold the strap snug with the part of your hand below your little fingers and with your first fingers and thumb do the strap ends right–over-left." Without looking up he asks Jeffrey, "Okay?"

"Yes, I'm following."

"Now, here's the most important part. Women and craftsmen skillfully pull the loose ends of the strap holding the strap in their first two fingers and their thumbs with their hands, palms down, facing the knot and then slide their hands away from the knot." The two look down at a perfect square knot.

The Choctaw elder breaks from his focus and looks at Jeffrey with a smile. "That's how we're taught. Draw with your forefingers and thumb," as he moves his hands in that motion.

Mitchell continues. "Men who are not craftsmen, who haven't been taught the right way, do it wrong. They do the last part with the ends held in their hands palms up then pull too quickly and too hard. It screws up the knot."

Agent Cooper lifts his eyesight from his focus on the knot, sits up in his chair and looks at Mitchell spellbound. "Thanks, that's amazing."

Mitchell responds: "And, better yet, with your wider flat leather strap it's even more obvious. Only a real skilled craftsman or woman ... someone who had a lot of practice, someone who is really focused, could do that," as he hands the strands with the square knot to Jeffrey.

Mitchell pauses, looks up at the sky and continues. "Jeffrey, here's another thing to prove this point. When men check or look at their fingernails they turn their hands palms up and close their fist. When women check their fingernails they open their hands palms down with their fingers fully extended. Just like the difference in men and women tying a square knot.

Jeffrey looks at his fingernails, palms up with a closed fist and chuckles slowly shaking his head and says, "Amazing, Uncle Mitchell. Now I'll never forget that one."

Mitchell grins.

"Uncle Mitchell, I've got a few more things, but should we take a break, have lunch?"

"No, I'd like to go through everything first," as he sits back in his chair. "Then we can see if there's anything we left out, talk about it at lunch. Besides, I can always open the jelly beans," he says smiling gleefully like a small child.

Agent Cooper stands up from his chair, stretches, and begins."The next item, how or what do you think they are using to knock these guys out, put them in a coma? There's no sign of drugs or knocking them out physically."

Mitchell quickly replies. "Okay, there are powders, even tiny injections, hard to detect, but most likely powders. If it's an Indian doing it, it's powders. They're made up of natural things like spider venoms and poisonous plants. They've been doing this for centuries. They have formulas for everything."

"How do they use them?"

"Mostly with a blow-reed filled with the powder, a three or maybe four inch long reed. I've seen them before, never used one. They blow the powder into their enemy's face or they might use a blow gun if they are farther away. It paralyses them almost immediately. Boom, down they go," Mitchell says this as he quickly moves both arms from his shoulder height to the ground.

"The Chickasaws are well-known for doing this, so are the Cherokee. They've been doing it for centuries. The only way you can detect it with most of them is to find the reed filled with the powder and take it apart."

Mitchell sits back in his chair again, pushes back and looks directly at Jeffrey. "The guys that use this stuff are really good. They have years of training, maybe a lifetime of training. They would be the best … only the best are allowed to use this stuff."

Agent Cooper stands up from his chair and walks around staying within a few steps of his chair. "Mitchell, I have a few more things; and I apologize that it's so much. It's that you've already been very helpful, and those of us trying to solve this incident are so lost."

"Jeffrey, this is great for me. It brings me back to so many things I've learned over the years. Oh! There's one more thing about those poison powders. You can't buy them. Some secretive tribal people make them. They use formulas that only they know. I'm not sure how they get them to the people who use them … but only a few people, even in the Indian world, have access to them."

Jeffrey holds his hand on his chin, looks around as though he is trying to store all of the information. He regains his focus. "Okay, this next item has to do with how they can move the men's bodies, the men being in a coma or stupor. How they can move them around and strap them to the trees. They're immobilized… like dead weight."

Mitchell looks up at the sky and slowly begins talking. "Jeffrey there's not much said about the intelligence of Indians, that's for sure," he says with a grin. He continues. "But think about it. How did our ancestors move fifty foot pine tree logs, sometimes eighty foot logs, to stand them upright as lodge poles to build a council house or that type of building? Look at the one at Mission San Louis, one of the most famous. It held over two thousand people inside. We don't think of these things other than that they existed. Think of the council houses built by the Creek Confederacy people. Indians are known to be experts with pulleys and fulcrums, just like the Aztecs and Egyptians. Indian ropes were made of plant and tree vines. Go to a large, mature forest with one hundred plus foot trees, you'll see thousands of vines, strong as cables. Just like Tarzan…They were good at using these like pulleys. Think of pulleys and fulcrums."

Agent Cooper sits back in his chair. "So, this is on a small scale but the knowledge of doing it is there."

"Yup, Jeffrey, let me add this. There's a story of guys working with large very heavy manhole covers. Wrestling them, using crow bars to lift them open then trying to roll them out of the way. Broken hands ... all that stuff. One of the men is an Indian who comes to work one day with a metal pole like a small flag pole with a chain and hook attached to the pole about half-way down. They got to where they needed to open a street manhole cover. The Indian guy gets out, takes the pole attached to the chain and hook, puts one end in one side of the manhole cover, puts the hook in the opposite side and lifts on the long end of the pole with one hand. Up comes the manhole cover. Then, he just moves it to the right or left and sets it down. An Indian built this. It's a simple fulcrum."

Agent Cooper leans forward in his chair. "So I can see some modern day MacGyver figuring out how to move these guys."

"I believe they're trained to do this," replies Mitchell. "Yup, I think they're trained. Remember too, most Indian men were pretty small, not six foot-two inches tall. More like five foot-six inches tall, and one hundred-thirty pounds at most. They needed to use leverage. We've always been good with fulcrums and pulleys."

Agent Cooper stood up again from his chair to stretch, then asks: "Given what we've talked about, the men being incoherent or in a coma, then tied to the trees the way they were, being bound with leather straps, the feathers ... Uncle Mitchell, if it is an Indian or Indians capturing them and doing this, what type of Indian would that be?"

Uncle Mitchell sits back in his chair then leans forward. "Jeffrey, I think it's a woman, maybe a man and a woman, maybe two women, but a woman for sure. She could be Creek, Chickasaw, or Cherokee. Maybe even Choctaw. But, yup, for sure it's a woman or two women. Yeah, I think the men wouldn't do this quite so well. Besides, mostly it's women who are trained for this. Indian lore talks about them like they are super human. In most southeastern Indian cultures women were the assassins and they did things like this. The men were warriors."

"Uncle Mitchell, what you're telling me is amazing. I don't know how to thank you."

"Jeffrey, I've lived in the Indian world all my life. Besides you don't need to thank me, you're my nephew. You're family."

The two look toward the trailer. "I'll go get Nina and the sandwiches," says Jeffrey as he strides toward the trailer.

Nina joins the two for lunch. There's nearly an hour of remembering family stories while the three enjoy jelly beans as dessert following the sandwiches.

As Agent Cooper and Nina drive away, Jeffrey looks back at the trailer in his rearview mirror, and then turns to look at Nina, "Nina, thank you for your help. I know how much you love Mitchell and respect him. He is truly a treasure. We're just leaving and I already miss him."

Nina smiles,"That's easy, Uncle Jeffrey. Just come more often."

Agent Cooper smiles and drives on.

Thirty minutes later Agent Cooper stops at a restaurant for coffee and to take time to compose and deliver an email message to Detective James and Federal Agent Gustafson.

1:20 pm, 24 January - Follow-Up from visit with Mitchell Ward, a Choctaw Indian elder.

Today I met with my uncle Mitchell Ward, approximately eighty-two years of age, at his home in rural Mississippi. Our meeting lasted approximately two hours including chit chat over lunch. He is known to me to be a Choctaw Indian elder very well informed and aware of the cultures and histories of Indians throughout the Southeastern United States. Mitchell is also a well-known Indian craftsman, known for his skills and knowledge by Indian peoples throughout Mississippi and adjacent states. We discussed four topics relevant to the current Biloxi sex trafficking case:

1. *The square knots – Precise, consistently perfect. Response – Characteristic of Indian craftsmen and women. Most likely done by a woman.*
2. *Doping or drugging of the three men into a stupor, immobilizing them – It was and is common in the southwestern Indian cultures to use powders delivered via hand-held reeds or blow guns. Historically, primarily administered by very skilled women or medicine men. This type of doping is still used today.*

3. *Moving, placing and arranging the men - Indians, like other ancient cultures were most often experts in the skill of moving objects with the use of fulcrum instruments and pulleys made from whatever resources were available. Mitchell believes there currently are highly-trained and skilled Indians who are trained in these skills including the movement of bodies.*

4. *His conclusion – Our suspect is a woman, perhaps two women, perhaps a woman and a man. But definitely a highly-trained woman is involved.*

I will be back in Biloxi in approximately two hours.

/s/ Jeffrey Cooper, Senior Agent, Mississippi Bureau of Investigation

Twelve

At the request of Detective James and Federal Agent Gustafson, they are joined by Agent Cooper and Police Chief Gavin at Chief Gavin's office. It's four thirty-five p.m. Agent Cooper has returned to Biloxi from his meeting with Choctaw elder Mitchell Ward.

Police Chief Gavin begins. "Agent Cooper, your e-mail is most interesting. I've read it several times and I'm beginning to believe it."

Federal Bureau Agent Gustafson moves to the edge of his seat. "I believe we'd better give it very strong consideration. This is a strange case, most likely unprecedented. Last night's false arrest was really based solely on weak … actually pathetic profiling. We can't afford to make any more mistakes. Somebody out there, some culprit, has us by the nuts. Detective James, what do you think?"

"I believe more and more in what Agent Cooper has discovered. It all fits. The first time I saw the nine square knots… all identical, absolutely identical. Then they're using three-eighth inch leather straps … not rope or twine. I knew it was something, or someone we'd never seen before. As far as the bodies…moving the doped men … yes, it's the best explanation so far, and yeah, these three guys are definitely doped with something nobody can figure out. I think we need to have the idea of an Indian woman suspect on our minds. If it's true, I'm not sure whether I'm more surprised or more impressed. It's like we're dealing with something or someone super human."

Federal Agent Gustafson moves from the edge of his seat to standing and pacing. Then he speaks, "How about if we start with looking at surveillance tapes. If we believe it's a woman, likely an athletic woman, we have the beginning of our profile. Let's get each casino hotel security team to look at their tapes for the times the three men were captured. I've got an assistant that could meet with the hotel security people if or when they find something suspicious."

"We have some tapes from the Bay St. Louis scene," says Detective James as he joins Agent Gustafson pacing around the room. He pauses. "Okay, we also have the vehicles, two of the vehicles, the Navigator and the Escalade. We can search the tapes from the parking garages for those vehicles, possibly those vehicles driven by a woman."

"Chief, let me make a suggestion," says Agent Gustafson. "I'll get my assistant over here from Mobile tonight. She and I can meet with each of the casino-hotel security chiefs first thing tomorrow to begin the search of the surveillance tapes."

Agent Cooper joins the standing two and speaks. "Agent Gustafson, I'll step in and help you coordinate the dates and possible locations. Ronnie and Chief Gavin, I'll need your help with that."

"Sounds good, I'll get my files and we can start as soon as we're through here. Chief, are you okay with that?" Detective James asks.

Chief Gavin joins in the conversation from his seat. "Ronnie, I suggest you have your assistant join you. Plus I've got another person that should be helpful. I'll get her over here right away."

Senior Agent Cooper looks around the room at the others. "Ronnie, I believe you said you've checked retailers for the leather straps. I'd guess not too many local retailers sell items like that. Have you checked the internet sales, places like Amazon or some specialty companies?"

"You're right, Jeffrey. There's nothing local. We've had an officer looking into it, but nothing here. Perhaps we can expand the search to New Orleans. I'll check again with my assistant to see what was found online."

Agent Cooper replies, "We have a lady in our Jackson office that has quite a bit of experience with that sort of thing. See who sells it; see who the buyers are. Maybe find a woman buyer."

Special Agent Gustafson joins the conversation. "I think we need to check it out, but it seems to me that if the person is a highly trained, likely underground connected person, the straps are coming directly from some Native American source...but I agree we need to check it out."

Chief Gavin works himself out of a slouch in his chair and speaks. "What else, Gentlemen?"

"I'd like to look into the pulley and fulcrum idea starting with any rock climbing gymnasiums for their body lifting equipment," says Agent Cooper. "We can look locally and online, like you're doing with the leather straps."

Detective James looks around the room, "We need anything we can find to develop a strong profile...this could be a real good start. Any and every clue is critical. Right now we have our best idea so far based on the evidence we have, but we still can't tie a person or persons to it. And, I agree with Agent Gustafson, we can't screw up with another false arrest."

Agent Gustafson looks around the room then steps back so he can see the other three. "Gentlemen, I think this is a good start. We've accepted Agent Cooper's work, and now we have the beginning of a plan for a new step in finding this culprit and solving this fiasco."

He pauses then continues. "Now that we have what's likely a good plan, let's put some meat on it."

Then he turns to look at Chief Gavin. "Chief, this should go without saying, but you need to have every available police officer and sheriff's deputy in the area on the hunt for any more of these 'nests.' Heaven help us if another one shows up handed to us by this person. If there are any more out there, your police force better be the one who finds them."

"I suggest we keep in touch tomorrow morning with any new thoughts or ideas we develop overnight then get together late morning or early afternoon," says Agent Cooper.

There is some nodding and mumbling of agreement among the others.

Thirteen

A north wind has followed a cold light rain. It's now a dry thirty-nine degrees, seven degrees above freezing. The residual moisture remains on the sidewalks and roadways leaving a hissing sound as car and truck tires cross the lightly wet blacktop. It's dark. A lone jogger is on his daily early morning run along the sidewalk paralleling U.S. Highway 90 south. His only focus outside the car and truck tire noise is his own rhythm: one-two-three-four, one-two-three-four, one-two-three-four, and one-two-three-four.

As his route comes within range of the familiar sound of the Biloxi lighthouse rotation, his mind transfers from his footsteps to the lighthouse, on-on-on-off; on-on-on-off; on-on-on-off; click – click – click – silent; click – click – click – silent; three-on, one-off; three-on, one-off; three-on, one-off. He smiles as he passes the area knowing the history of the lighthouse clicking sound. As he passes the lighthouse pattern, he's suddenly startled. He jumps back. There's something or someone moving ahead, shuffling, then suddenly moaning. He can barely see a shadow of something at the Old French Biloxi Cemetery area just ahead. It's still too dark to see clearly at this winter hour.

The object and sound become louder and clearer as he cautiously steps closer, his upper body leading the way. The morning darkness and cold breeze keep the sight and sound difficult. "What in hell!" he blurts out," as he sees what appears to be a person in the darkness. His words and voice seem to echo as he looks around to see if anyone or anything has joined him.

Moments later he speaks in aloud whisper, "Holy shit. It is a person."

He reminds himself, *'Glen stay back … don't go any closer … be ready to run … back up a few steps,'* as his upper body leans away from the object.

His hands shake as he retrieves his cell phone then fumbles to dial nine-one-one. Just as the operator responds he hears a muffled yell coming from the indiscernible person or object. "Operator, there's a person, I'm pretty sure it's a person on the sidewalk at the gate at the Old French Biloxi Cemetery on Beach."

"Sir," the operator replies, "Don't go any closer. Are you there alone?"

"Yeah, operator, it's just me," as he slowly looks around. "I'm jogging and I see this… this something moving ahead of me. Then I hear a moaning and other noise, like they're trying to say or yell something. It's cold and wet from last night's rain. Guess that's why I'm the only one out jogging right now…scared the shit out of me!"

"Sir, I have a call into the police. You're at the Beach Boulevard gate at the Old French Biloxi Cemetery, correct?"

"Yes, operator."

"Sir, the police will be there shortly. Their headquarters is just around the corner a few blocks from you. There should be an officer there shortly. I'm going to stay on the line with you 'til the police arrive."

"Thanks. It's really cold out here."

"Okay, let me see if they can get another car out there so you can get inside and get warm."

"Thanks ... Okay, I hear the police siren and see the police car's lights ... And, I can see the person better now with the police car lights shining on it. I can see now, it's definitely a person. Holy shit! It looks like he's on his knees tied with his back to the fence, like he's impaled to the fence. Okay, the police officer is here. Thanks operator."

Police Officer Milford arrives at the scene and cautiously walks over to the person and immediately calls headquarters. "Hey, Officer Milford here, I'm at the Old French Biloxi Cemetery gate and there's a man ... looks like he's tied to the front gate on southbound 90. Looks like the other ones we found hogtied, he's mumbling something, then lets out a scream. I'll need help, plus you need to get the detective out here."

"I'll get hold of the Chief and Detective James right away. There is another police officer on the way to help, we'll get a third. Be careful Officer Milford."

A second police officer arrives shortly. "Officer Milford, right?"

"Yes. Glad you're here."

"I'm Neil Lee."

"Neil, can you get a statement from the guy standing behind us. He's the one who found the guy tied to the gate and called nine-one-one. He's freezing his ass off if you can put him in your car, and get him a blanket?"

"Got it. You okay? I can call in another officer."

"Thanks, but the detective should be here any minute. This guy is really messed up. It looks like he's staring at a monster or something, shaking like a leaf in a hurricane. I'll get the area taped off while we're waiting for the detective."

*   *   *

Detective Ronnie James arrives and introduces himself to Officer Milford as he cautiously begins to inspect the man strapped to the gate.

"Milford, we'd better get another officer here, maybe two more," Detective James instructs. "I've got Jan Snow coming to do photos...she should be here any minute. We will need help taking pictures and we need to deal with people stopping to see what's going on. This will likely draw a crowd real soon."

Immediately after making the call, Officer Milford begins following closely behind Detective James.

"Milford, we need to be careful. This guy is worse than the others. It looks like he's not going to like for us to touch him. I've never seen anybody shake like this. When the paramedics get here we'll see if they can give him a shot or something."

As the detective steps back and focuses his flashlight on the man's face, he shakes his head and says to Milford, "Look at this. He's just staring straight ahead, his pupils are wide open ... they don't close when the light is shining on them."

Detective James continues his inspection while he explains what he is seeing to Officer Milford. "Okay, see how he's on his knees with his legs tied together at the back of the gate?"

"Yeah, I see. That's got to hurt."

"Same with the upper arms. Plus, if you look closely the knots are all perfect square knots, same as the other three men we found like this."

Police photographer Jan Snow arrives and she immediately begins taking photographs of the man strapped to the gate and the scene surrounding him.

Detective James removes a note from the elastic of the screaming man's underwear and hands it to Officer Milford. "Milford, hang on to that. Call headquarters with the address written on the note. Tell them I've asked you to call it in. Need to get SWAT over to the address right just like they did with the first three. They'll call the chief to alert SWAT. Have them call me if they need to."

*   *   *

 As the paramedics arrive, Detective James instructs the police officers and growing crowd, "Make room for the paramedics. Stay out of their way so they can do their job."

The first paramedic jumps out of the driver's side of the ambulance and quickly steps directly in front of the man strapped to the cemetery gate. He looks at the man next to him and says, "Hi, I'm Ernie. You're Detective James from the other night, right?"

Detective James continues to focus on the man then replies. "Yeah, that's me. I'm just trying to finish up. I need to get some light on his back and the knots, and then Miss Snow will need your help with a few photos of his head and neck area."

"Ernie, we might need your partner to help with the pictures of the head area then we can cut him loose. Be careful, this guy looks and sounds mean…he's got to be really high on something."

As they continue Ernie asks. "Detective, who do you think is doing this?"

"Don't know, but one of the agents working on this with us thinks it could be a woman, probably an Indian, a Native American woman. Keep that under your hat for now, but Ernie, we just don't know yet."

As they're cutting the straps and the two paramedics work to strap the man to the stretcher, Ernie looks up at Detective James and says, "My sister is into martial arts. She's five- foot-four, I'm six-foot."

He stops and says to his paramedic partner, "Hold on a minute, I've got to tell the detective something. So, we're at a family picnic a few weeks ago. My sister wanted to show off I guess … tells me to pretend I was going to steal her purse. Five seconds later, I'm flying through the air… land on my ass. Flipped me right through the air! Yup, I can believe a woman could do this."

Detective James breaks his concentration for a brief moment and looks up at the paramedic. "Okay, thanks Ernie. You'd better get going and get this guy out of here. The news people are already circling."

"Right sir, we're going to the hospital just up the street."

Detective James' phone rings. "Ronnie, its Chief Gavin. Am I to believe what I'm hearing?"

"Yes, Chief, I'm afraid so. I've got to stop at the hospital for a few minutes then I'll come over to your office. Oh! Chief, SWAT needs to get over to the address we called in. It was just called in a few minutes ago."

"Right, I got the call. They're on their way. See you shortly."

Chief Gavin walks over to the coffee area, pours another cup then walks slowly back to his desk as he sits down and begins to stare at the ceiling.

*　　*　　*

Detective James surveys the cemetery gate area and the crime scene. As he watches the police vehicles and media leave, he scans the boulevard and the long, flat sand beach greeting the dawn. With a deep breath of the cold morning air, he grasps the front of his coat collar to keep out the cold. He does a final three hundred sixty degree scan of the scene then says to himself, "Looks more-and-more like Agent Cooper's Indian elder might be right. If he's right the woman or women who put this plan together to capture, disable and display these pimps, then guide us to their young women victims are incredibly well-trained, disciplined and clever. This is not going to be easy."

He walks briskly to his car trying to prepare for what will likely be another tortuous day.

*   *   *

At eight forty-five a.m. Mayor Williams sends an URGENT MESSAGE via text and e-mail to be accompanied by a follow up telephone call from his staff to the leading law enforcement personnel involved in these cases, requesting each one to meet this morning to learn the facts of the new incident and further, to prepare for a three-thirty p.m. news conference to be held at city hall regarding this new incident and an update on the previous three.

Fourteen

Biloxi Mayor, Mike Williams, and City Attorney, Mark Acres are seated in the mayor's office waiting to view the morning television news.

"Mark, let's watch this report then make our call to the governor."

Nodding his agreement, Mark Acres said "When I drove past the police headquarters on my way here. There are already a handful of major media vehicles with towers out there."

The television screen suddenly flashes 'URGENT UPDATE' accompanied by a high-decibel dramatic sound bite.

"Good morning and welcome to our update regarding the sex trafficking case and other news from the eight o'clock morning news live from the Gulf Coast. I'm Harold Cunningham."

A second newscaster anxiously follows. "And, I'm Marcie Vincent. We're here with more breaking news. As we speak, several media companies have gathered at the Biloxi Police Headquarters building in response to the fourth incident involving sex trafficking here in Biloxi. Our on-site reporter Craig Wilson is live at the scene. Craig, we're just now seeing your camera man's live video streaming. Can you give us an update?"

"Yes, Marcie. Good morning. This place is becoming a media zoo. As we look around we see five major network's equipment. Another one is just turning in to the parking area. We're awaiting an announcement from the police regarding the fourth incident that took place last night or early this morning where another man was found bound and tied, this time to the Biloxi Old French Cemetery front gate."

The reporter pauses as he shuffles his notes then continues. "There is no report of the man's condition. In addition, apparently the police found a note on the man that led the Biloxi SWAT team to raid another house where they discovered more young women. Again, Marcie, we do not have details regarding that raid and hope to be briefed on that shortly."

"Craig, this is Harold Cunningham, have there been any sightings of the mayor, police chief, or any other city officials?"

"No, Harold, we've just had one of the deputies come out to the press area and advise us that there would be an update, hopefully within the next half hour."

"Craig, thanks."

"Oh, and Harold, as we were talking it looks like two more media tower-vehicles have arrived. I'll have our camera man scan over there."

"Okay, Craig. We're prepared to cut into our program when you have any news, especially the update from the police. Now, other news will follow right after our break."

*   *   *

Mayor Williams looks at Mark Acres, pauses then says, "Mark, I'd like for you to handle the media update over at the police headquarters. I have to make a call to the governor. I'll try to connect you to the call, but make your control of the media discussion your first priority."

*   *   *

Attorney Acres steps up to the press podium at the police headquarters media area. He is unaccompanied.

"Ladies and gentlemen, today is another truly tragic day for our great city. At six-thirty this morning a local jogger was on his daily run heading south on the sidewalk running parallel to the south bound lane of Beach Boulevard when he discovered an object or something that he thought might be a person at the Biloxi Old French Cemetery gate. Still dark, he called nine-one-one who immediately dispatched a Biloxi police officer. They discovered a man, incoherent, strapped to the street side of the cemetery gate. Additional Biloxi police officers and detectives were called to the scene. The strapped man was taken to the local hospital where he remains in critical condition."

He pauses as he looks out at the audience of anxious news reporters and camera men.

"This man, like three others before him, had a note tucked into his underwear elastic that led the police to a house in Biloxi. The Biloxi SWAT team surrounded the house, broke through the front door and arrested a man and an adult woman, and found seven young women believed to be being used for prostitution."

Several reporters begin shouting questions.

Attorney Acres responds. "Let me finish please ... and no, I cannot answer any questions at this time. Obviously, this will take time to sort through. It's the fourth event. Our staffs are all overwhelmed. Our top priority is to take care of the young women. There is an all-out manhunt for the person or persons who have captured and drugged the four men. There is also an all-out search for any other sex trafficking and prostitution in Biloxi and the nearby areas. Finally, I'll ask that you each give us your patience and help in any way. We will announce when our next briefing will be from this podium."

Attorney Acres steps away from the podium then walks back into the police headquarters building.

Mayor Williams immediately calls Attorney Acres.

"Mark, good job with the briefing, I just got off the phone with the governor. He is preparing to offer us help from the state. I hope to hell he's not going to declare Biloxi in a state of emergency. Can you come over to my office to discuss what we need to do? I told him we would call when you had joined me in my office."

"Sir, I'm on my way."

*   *   *

"Thanks for getting here so quickly, Mark."

As Attorney Acres settles into his seat, he turns to the mayor. "Mayor Williams, this fourth episode just set everything off. It's like a volcanic eruption. The media coverage has hit the international level. There's even a tower truck out there representing the BBC Corporation. I guess they must be stationed in New Orleans? Anyway, this whole situation is really out of hand at this point."

"I agree. Mark." Mayor Williams rubs his chin and slowly shakes his head side-to-side. "Okay, Mark, we need to go ahead and make the call to the governor...see what he is thinking."

Following the introductions and preliminary bits of conversation, Governor Copeland begins. "Gentlemen, given the situation in Biloxi, as governor, I'm considering specific actions to be taken by the state. We have determined that your situation has not reached the magnitude of declaring a state of emergency. However, I'm offering and insisting on your cooperation in having the State of Mississippi take full charge and responsibility for the care and handling of the twenty-plus young women who are caught up in this quagmire. We will provide for their housing, health care, legal representation, safety and security. Of course, it will be done in coordination with your existing medical team and other professionals."

Mayor Acres and Attorney Acres nod agreement to each other.

The governor continues. "In addition, we will provide full use of our legal assets to these women, plus to your office. And, we realize your police department is understaffed, even under normal conditions. We will make available significant numbers of police personnel and resources, including the Mississippi State Police and the Mississippi Bureau of Investigation assets and personnel. You should receive an e-mail copy of the official letter detailing this in a few minutes. I'd like to make a formal news conference announcement regarding this at one o'clock this afternoon."

Attorney Acres responds. "Governor, we'll need to have the okay of the city council. Mayor Williams and I will expedite this with a conference call to them, then call and follow up our response to you in writing."

The governor replies. "Mayor Williams and Attorney Acres, we have a mess to handle and clean up. My greatest concern is that your city and county facilities cannot handle the needs of these twenty-five young women, perhaps with more to come. We have the physical and financial means to do this. Quite frankly, you don't."

Again, the mayor and city attorney nod their agreement to each other.

Governor Copeland speaks again. "The other comment I have is that this takes everyone's greatest concern off your hands ... it lets you focus on finding the person or persons capturing and displaying these men. Then we all need to continue to work at cleaning up the prostitution and sex trafficking. My goal is to help you do that and end this tragedy."

"Governor, its Mike Williams. I believe Attorney Acres and I are in agreement with your offer. We'll review the letter as soon as we end this call. I'll repeat what Attorney Acres said, we'll conference call the city council members to get their agreement. We'll be back on the phone with you immediately after that. And, governor, thank you."

*   *   *

Following a conference call to city council members from Mayor Williams and City Attorney Acres, Mayor Williams advises Governor Copeland of the city's agreement to proceed with the matters discussed earlier. The mayor then instructs his staff to advise each of the lead persons involved in the sex trafficking case that Mississippi Governor Copeland has scheduled a one o'clock broadcast. Further, that an emergency two-thirty p.m. meeting to be attended by persons as invitees only, that the meeting will be held at a location to be announced privately to each participant, that invitee participants will be advised of the location at one-thirty, and that a three-thirty p.m. press conference would take place at the police headquarters press area in the format of a prepared speech.

*   *   *

Mark Acres and Mayor Williams are seated in the Mayor's office. The television screen flashes 'URGENT SEX TRAFFICKING UPDATE' again accompanied by high-decibel audio and clips of the scene at Bay St. Louis, Treasure Bay Casino and the motor cycle led police car brigade delivering the two falsely arrested men to police headquarters.

Cameras focus on the first announcer. "Good afternoon and welcome to our special broadcast from the Governor's Office in Jackson, Mississippi where the governor is expected to make an announcement regarding the Biloxi sex trafficking case. I'm Harold Cunningham."

The camera switches to the co-broadcaster. "And, I'm Marcie Vincent. We're about to see a live telecast from Mississippi Governor Copeland regarding what has become an internationally broadcast tragedy taking place here on our Gulf Coast."

The scene is now on the governor seated at his desk. An announcer starts the presentation by introducing him: "Ladies and Gentlemen, the Governor of the State of Mississippi, Lawrence Copeland."

The governor follows.

"In August 2005, eleven and one-half years ago, Hurricane Katrina charged ashore leaving our great City of Biloxi, most of the Mississippi Gulf Coast and much of the rest of the state in near ruins. The damage and destruction was beyond imagination. Hundreds of people lost their lives and millions lost their homes, businesses and jobs. The damage and destruction was beyond imagination. With our men and women accompanied by companies and corporations from around the world, plus federal, state and local resources, we fought back; we fought back hard. We made our Gulf Coast communities and the City of Biloxi great again.

We are now faced with a very difficult situation in the City of Biloxi and nearby areas. One of the most heinous crimes of the human race; the kidnapping, raping, enslaving and sex trafficking of young women, has infested our great city and great state. My greatest concern is for the immediate and long term care of the twenty-five enslaved young women.

As governor, I, along with the unanimous approval of my cabinet members, have given consideration of specific actions to be taken by the government of the State of Mississippi. Following conversations with Biloxi Mayor Mike Williams and Biloxi City Attorney Mark Acres, along with the unanimous agreement of the Biloxi City Council, we agree that the State of Mississippi will immediately take full charge and responsibility for the care and handling of the twenty-five young women, and possibly more, caught up in this tragedy. We will immediately move to provide for their housing, health care, including trauma and mental health care. Further, we will provide legal representation, all safety and security measures necessary during their recuperation and rehabilitation. This will be in full conjunction with the existing health care, legal and other professionals.

The State of Mississippi will make available significant numbers of police personnel and resources including the Mississippi State Police and the Mississippi Bureau of Investigation assets and personnel to help resolve the four existing cases and any others that might occur. We have committed resources for the manhunt for the person who has captured, disabled, and made messengers of the four men each involved in the four cases.

With that, I thank all of the men and women, companies and agencies for their involvement and assistance in this matter. May God Bless the great City of Biloxi and the great State of Mississippi."

*   *   *

"Mark, I think it was a good idea and a good speech."

"So do I mayor, I think we should be grateful for the idea of involving the state the way he did. Let's hope it works out and works out quickly."

"I'll make the call to the governor thanking him, then let's you and I get to work on plans for the two-thirty." Mayor Williams hesitates then continues while looking up at Attorney Acres. "I see, Mark, that I've just received a note from the governor that Lieutenant Governor Shannessy will be here for our two-thirty meeting."

Attorney Acres looks down at the floor while remaining in his seated position then slowly looks up at the mayor, "Ah, yes! Lieutenant Governor John Shannessy. This should be interesting."

Fifteen

The sound of chairs being shuffled into formation, along with the chatter of the staff, breaks the silence at the large open rooftop pool area. It's the last step in setting up the canopy covered area of the eleventh story at Biloxi's IP Casino and Hotel. The last minute request from Mayor Mike Williams has been met with urgency.

The secluded open outdoor pool area with its stunning eleventh floor panoramic view of Biloxi, the Biloxi beaches and the Gulf of Mexico has a history of memorable corporate and municipal gatherings and events. The rooftop area is closed for the winter season, so it's an ideal venue for the two-thirty meeting closed to the public. Police and IP Hotel security guards are in place at the elevator entrances and exits. These elevators are the only way to access the eleventh floor with the exception of the three emergency stairways. Security guards are in place at each of the stairway exits as well. Each security guard and police officer assigned to this duty has a list of the selected attendees. Each of the security personnel is authorized to request appropriate identification from those invitees.

Shuffling continues as the IP staff complete the meeting seating arrangement, placing outdoor heating equipment to accommodate the January weather, and the last minute testing of the sound system with the podium set at a low decibel level, loud enough for the audience, yet inaudible beyond the designated area.

*   *   *

Biloxi City Attorney Mark Acres steps to the podium to open the scheduled meeting as the last three stragglers are seated. The group of invitees sits in total silence as he begins:

"Welcome, ladies and gentlemen. I'm Biloxi City Attorney Mark Acres. Governor Copeland requested Mayor Williams and I assemble this meeting of invitees only to share the information we have, share our thoughts and plans, and gain all your thoughts to develop plans going forward. Per the governor's broadcast message an hour-and-a-half ago, Mayor Williams and our city council have agreed to follow the first aspect of these plans, that of caring for the twenty-five young women. Per this agreement, these women are now under the care of the State of Mississippi and its designated representatives. At this time I'll turn the meeting over to Mississippi Lieutenant Governor John Shannessy."

Lieutenant Governor Shannessy steps up to the podium.

"Governor Copeland asked me to be here today to present his plan to help with the care of the twenty-five young women … hopefully not more. He also asked me to meet with Mississippi Bureau of Investigation Senior Agent Jeffrey Cooper and ask him to speak on behalf of the combined state, federal and local law enforcement groups regarding their efforts and plans. He has agreed. Senior Agent Cooper has been a part of this investigation for several days and has been an integral part of the work and investigation that has taken place. Finally, the governor has asked the local Prosecuting Attorney John Darlson along with the Mississippi Assistant State Attorney General Megan Duncan to discuss and lead ongoing efforts regarding the prosecution of the men and one woman who are accused and being held on a number of charges including abducting, kidnapping, raping and trafficking for prostitution, along with interstate trafficking of the twenty-five, possibly more, young women. The governor has asked the two of us to lead the discussion today regarding that aspect of the case."

The lieutenant governor looks back and forth viewing the audience. "The thirty-seven persons, each of us called to this assembly, carries a burden and an opportunity to save these young women from the tragedies put upon them. We carry the responsibility of helping them regain their lives. The governor and assistant state attorney general have asked Doctor Rachel Larsen of the Harrison County Office of the Mississippi State Health Department to assemble a team of professionals to work with these young victims. Doctor Larsen has been an integral leader since the onset of this tragedy. Doctor Larsen, please come on up and introduce yourself."

The Doctor steps to the podium. "Thank you all for being here. And, thank you to Governor Copeland and Lieutenant Governor Shannessy for taking on this role on behalf of the twenty-five...and I hope and pray no more, young women. We are awaiting news of the location and facilities for these victims to be transferred to. And, yes, we are really struggling to keep things together and keep on track to care for these women. We have been assured that the facility will be available within forty-eight hours. Until that time, we ask for your continued support and your prayers for our staff and the young women victims."

Lieutenant Governor Shannessy stands from his seat and without going to the podium, announces, "Next, Mississippi Bureau of Investigation Senior Agent Jeffrey Cooper. Jeffrey, could you please step up to the podium and give us an update?"

Agent Cooper begins while walking to the podium.

"Thank you, sir. I'll be brief. Yesterday I was part of a group who met to discuss what we could do as a team to find the person or persons who has or have captured the pimps and put them on display before notifying us of where to find these young women victims. At that time, late yesterday afternoon, there were three such incidents. Now there is a fourth."

" The group who met yesterday afternoon included senior members of the Biloxi Police Department, Special Agent Gustafson from the Federal Bureau of Investigation, and me. Yesterday morning I met with a Native American elder whom I believe to be very knowledgeable about Native American, especially southeastern Indian, culture. Based on an extensive conversation with him, he is convinced that what has taken place in capturing and disabling these men has been done by southeastern Indians, most likely a woman or women. The incident last night or this morning with the man strapped to the cemetery gate gives further confirmation of this. The group determined that they would all fully support a search for this profile and would further encourage a massive hunt for any more women being held in captivity for prostitution. We have called upon all local, state and federal agencies to help in a variety of capacities. I'll end with that."

As Agent Cooper turns to resume his seat, an attendee stands and addresses him.

"Sir, Agent Cooper, I'm Sylvia Shannessy. I am the wife of the lieutenant governor. I traveled here early this morning and met with several of these young women. Please explain how this person who you believe is a Native American woman, has identified these pimps ... these monsters. She has abducted them, drugged them with an indiscernible substance before leaving them in a nearly brain dead condition, stripped them of most of their clothing, then neatly tied and left them in such public locations. Explain how this person or these two people knew where these pimps, these despicable monsters were, where they live and what their business is, while your entire police force, the county sheriffs, and your state police officers, knew nothing about this sick businesses, occurring I believe right under their noses."

As she pauses, Agent Cooper looks over at Lieutenant Governor Shannessy who shrugs his shoulders, smiles, and says, "Sylvia, go ahead and finish, but be brief."

"Okay, we now have over two dozen girls who have been abused beyond any of our imaginations. One young victim I met has written: 'I woke naked, in a daze in an unfamiliar place. My seventeen-year-old body was sore, my arms were bruised, and my vagina was burning with pain. I had bite marks on my neck and entire upper body. A vaguely familiar man was standing over me, looking down at me as I lay naked. He said, "I'm Michael. Do you remember me from last night?" My body turned into a tight fetal position, my lips trembled and I hid my face from him. I told him I want to go home; don't touch me anymore. He sat on the edge of the bed and said, "Your name is Stephanie, right?" I didn't answer. "Stephanie, we're in a place far from your home. You live here now. We'll bring you food in a little while. You can't escape. Soon you'll realize you live in a much nicer place than you came from, nice clothes, all the things you've dreamed of." All I could think of was how much I missed my Mom, my sisters Jennie and Alice, my brother Ray, all my friends on the volleyball team, my dog, my chickens, my house. I just want to go home. Please help us, and please help our sisters and friends so this doesn't happen to them.'"

Once again she looks around the room filled with stunned invitees, some with tears in their eyes. She speaks again, "This isn't a situation, and this isn't an incident. This is a tragedy. And, finally, let me finish, thank God for the person you believe you're looking for... this Native American woman or these two people who so courageously captured these pimps, these despicable monsters, rendered them helpless and put them on display, then guided the police to these beautiful young women saving their lives. I say to whomever she or they are, God bless you, and thank you for your service."

As Sylvia returns to her seat, the lieutenant governor graciously thanks her while a distinct humming noise rises from the attendees. Amidst the distraction, he turns to Prosecuting Attorney John Darlson and speaks. "The final leg of our mission is the prosecution of the now nine men and one woman believed to be the persons who abducted and kidnapped these women and brought them to Biloxi. Prosecuting Attorney John Darlson has been chosen to lead the group prosecuting these nine people. John!"

Darlson walks to the podium in his familiar deliberate gait and begins his presentation with his trademark soft, deliberate tone and pace. "Thank you all for putting the trust in me to carry out this difficult task. I'm humbled to be in front of you today. The challenge for each and every one of us assembled here today is huge. From my standpoint it involves the intense prosecution of nine suspected criminals, eight men and one woman, for crimes that fall under local, state and federal judicial jurisdictions. Second, the crimes committed are among the most heinous and require the most meticulous gathering of evidence to achieve the harshest punishments they deserve. Some of them reach the level of capital punishment, the death penalty. The twenty-five or more young women will need all of our care and patience in helping us convict these disgusting people. In discussions with my staff, the State of Mississippi prosecutors, and the federal prosecutors, we are most pleased with the actions taken today by the governor. We pray that no more incidents take place in this great city. We pray too for everyone involved to have great patience and great personal strength. We pray most of all for the twenty-five young women. Thank you."

The lieutenant governor stands from his seat and speaks loudly over the shuffling and murmur of the crowd. "Folks, thanks for being here today, we have contact information for each of you. Please be alert to any further events and please work in any way you can with local, state and federal officials using your expertise. Let's all get back to work."

Sixteen

I'm sitting at a table in the first floor IP lobby coffee shop watching several of the two-thirty special meeting attendees walk past. I'm dressed ready for travel in my fitness clothes with an additional short-waist exercise jacket to accommodate the January weather. My mission is complete. As the parade of government agents and employees, and other meeting attendees pass by, some with a semi-urgent gait, others meandering, and a few moving at a Darlson-like pace, I amuse myself with a soft smile and the thought, *'It takes all these people and more to take over where I left off.'*

Twenty-five minutes later, I'm driving west on Interstate Ten. Destination: New Orleans. I'm using the pseudonym Kathy Shay during the New Orleans visit. I'll make a quick stop at the Louisiana Welcome Center to deliver the coded message *'Mission Complete'* to the contact for the group I contracted with to perform and fulfill the mission. My second stop is the Louis Armstrong New Orleans International Airport to exchange the rental car I've been driving for the car provided by a north Florida Indian tribe. I'll exchange this car for my own at the tribe's headquarters next week on my way back to my home in Jacksonville.

*   *   *

My arrival at the final destination, the Hilton Riverwalk registration area, is right on schedule ... six o'clock. I feel myself breaking out in a smile while looking around the second floor mezzanine area waiting to register. I love this place. I'm here for me...just to treat myself following the incredibly successful mission. Just to know I saved the twenty-five young women from disaster and to give them a second chance at life.

The person in the registration line behind me, a well-dressed middle age man with his businessman's suitcase, taps me on the back of my shoulder and says in a quiet voice with a soft southern accent, "Miss, you're next. The receptionist just called for you."

I turn and with a nod, a quick smile, and, "Thanks" as I hurry to the receptionist's station.

A pleasant welcome comes from a young Asian-looking woman stationed behind the registration counter dressed in her tan Hilton suit. It reminds me of my previous job at the Biloxi Beau Rivage registration area.

"Yes, I have a reservation. It's Kathy Shay," as I hand her my ID and a credit card.

"Thank you Miss Shay. I have you staying with us for three nights, is that correct?"

"Yes."

"Miss Shay, you have an incredible smile. Are you here with someone?"

I feel myself blushing and stumble to reply, "Oh...no, just me. Honestly, I'm here by myself." I guess I wasn't expecting the question.

As the receptionist completes her work for my registration, I beam and say, "I guess I'm smiling so much because I just finished a very difficult job. Plus I love this place."

"I'm sorry, I didn't mean...."

I have to smile, feeling what she must be thinking. "It's fine. Don't worry...I'm fine."

"Okay, Miss Shay. I have you pre-paid for three nights. Your room is adjacent to the Mark Twain Courtyard as you requested. Just one key, right?" she says with a smile.

"Just one key," I nod, again.

As I leave the receptionist area and walk toward my room, I cross the railway overpass leading to the hotel area and my room. The railway overpass walkway is the site of my successful kill of Mr. Goetz last year. I stop in my tracks as I visualize the moment like it has just happened. I take a deep breath as I look down at the carpeted floor; then continue the walk to my room.

Once in my room, it's time to unpack, and take a long run along the riverfront. It will be my meditation for the day.

The riverfront run is one of my favorites. Today it gives me a chance to clear my mind of the past week's events.

When I return to my room, it's time of a quick shower, and then it's down to Drago's. I'm hoping for a front row seat at the oyster bar for a cup of Mama Ruth's Gumbo and enjoying the charbroiled oyster and fresh oyster shucking show. One of the best parts of the visit is watching the patrons, the oyster shuckers, and the cooks having a good time.

As I walk to the shower, my mind is rambling. *'Maybe the receptionist has the right idea. Maybe … just maybe, I'll meet someone at the oyster bar. Maybe the businessman with the great southern voice and accent will be there … Maybe not. Get going, Cowart. Take your shower and get going. It's night-time in New Orleans.'*

*   *   *

The night at the oyster bar was good, but mostly uneventful. I find sitting at the bar rather than being seated alone at a table at an upscale restaurant so much more entertaining. Tonight during the two hours there I met four people, all tourists; two were New Orleans experienced, two first time visitors. The most fun was the horseradish farmer from Missouri. A little too much to drink, but he shared great stories. He even went to his room and brought me a sample of their fresh homemade stuff. Of course, I had to sample it while we were there. He and his wife were overjoyed when I shared with the oyster shucker and the lady sitting next to me on my other side. It was all good!

Plans for tomorrow are simple. Yoga here, a trolley ride to Jackson Square, followed with coffee and beignets at Café du Monde. Then I'll walk it off by spending the rest of the day at the square and touring the art shops. I'll visit Fulton Street on my way back to the hotel. Finally, back to the hotel for evening chardonnay overlooking the Mississippi from the open Mark Twain courtyard, watching the ships from around the world navigate the Mississippi's famous New Orleans crescent, seeing the skyline and stars overhead.

*   *   *

The day starts with an eye opener. The New Orleans News had broadcast a breaking story headline regarding with an update on the sex trafficking case in Biloxi.

I'm glued to the television in my room as the news reporter introduces the Biloxi, 'News at eight from the Gulf Coast' and the familiar face of Marcie Vincent. She begins. "We have news from earlier this morning that the police have surrounded a house in Ocean Springs, immediately east of Biloxi. According to our sources, we're told that the house is believed to be the home of the mystery woman believed to be the person or one of the persons who captured and disabled the men in the sex trafficking cases. We'll bring you updated news as soon as it is available."

The second broadcast person continues, "Marcie, this adds a whole new element to this already incredible story."

"Yes, Harold it does. We'll be back with an update on this significant event as soon as further news is available."

"Am I ever glad I'm in New Orleans!" I blurt out. "I know one thing, they won't find anything there." Getting dressed, I head out for the trolley and Café du Monde, a tour of the square and shops, then lunch at Cafe Pontalba.

*   *   *

A thin gray-haired man with a neatly groomed beard, dressed in a gold-colored vest, black slacks and a white waiter's cloth over his left arm meets me at the café entrance. "Welcome to Café Pontalba. Are you meeting someone?"

"No, just one. And, sir, I'd like to be seated where I have a view of the television news and, if possible, the square in front of the entrance to the cathedral."

"Actually, Miss, if you sit at the corner of the bar, it will accommodate both."

"Well, thank you. That's perfect," I say with a nod and a smile.

The gentleman escorts me to the bar and helps me with the bar seat then with a slight bow politely says, "The bartender can take your order for food and beverages."

I have a great view of the street intersection between the café and the cathedral. I recall breaking one guy's nose and breaking another guy's leg when I was here with my college friends … Shay was one of them. I remember the four of us running from the scene leaving one man lying face down in a pool of blood, the other screaming as he looked at his leg sideways from the knee down, so much for the two of them groping women. That was how many years ago? I think I was in my second year of training.

Suddenly, the television grabs my attention as I see the 'Breaking News' stripe flash on followed by the familiar face of Marcie Vincent. Following the dramatic introduction she begins. "Noon news from the Gulf Coast has learned that the police have found and searched a house in Ocean Springs where they believe the Biloxi sex trafficking mystery woman has lived for the past four months. The search operation was headed by the Mississippi State Police. Their spokesperson did state that the name of the person suspected could not be given out at this time, however our sources say the house was rented to a 'Nancy Cole,' and that she is the person believed to be responsible for the four cases of capturing, disabling, and displaying the men in such a public manner. Each of the men had a note attached to his clothing providing the address of a house where the twenty-five young women were found. Harold, there's more…"

"Yes, I'm Harold Cunningham with more on the story. The police spokesperson stated that the house was found empty of any personal belongings, and that it has been, and continues to be searched for fingerprints, DNA, and other personal evidence. The person, named, 'Nancy Cole,' is believed to be Native American, likely a member of an underground American Indian organization whose mission is to protect the rights of American Indians and impose revenge against persons who violate their rights and are not otherwise held responsible or punished for their crimes."

Marcie Vincent continues. "According to our sources fourteen of the twenty-five young women rescued in the sex trafficking case are Native American. We have a tape of an interview conducted less than an hour ago with a representative of the women who are victims of the Biloxi sex trafficking. Let's go ahead with the tape."

"I'm Craig Wilson for Gulf Coast News and I have with me Attorney Mazie Rossell who represents the fourteen Native American women. Mrs. Rossell, can you bring us up to date with your work with these young women and other aspects of this case?"

"Yes, first of all, I have no knowledge of this person whose house was found and raided, or of any person who participated in capturing, putting the men in a stupor, displaying them, and then leading the police to find these young women. Whoever you are, God bless you, and thank you for what you have done. I can tell you that I represent fourteen young Native American women and three others, so seventeen of the twenty-five. I have been advised by representatives of the State of Mississippi that all twenty-five are being transported to an undisclosed, secure facility in Mississippi where they will receive full attention of the state and federal governments, and several Native American tribes during their rehabilitation. I'll add, this is an enormous task and I'm thankful for Governor Copeland for taking charge of this."

Reporter Wilson completes the taping with, "Thank you Mrs. Rossell. Now back to the news."

Marcie Vincent is back on the screen. "Howard, have we heard anything from the Biloxi police or the mayor's office?"

"No, Marcie, we have not. We believe there will be an announcement from the governor's office sometime this afternoon or evening."

"Thanks again, Harold. Now to other news.

*   *   *

Yesterday leaders of eleven southeastern Indian tribes summoned senior officials of the Bureau of Indian Affairs and the United States Department of Interior to an emergency meeting to be held at the Mississippi Band of Choctaw Indians Reservation. The topic and message:

WITH UTMOST URGENCY.

To review plans to usurp the announcement of plans mandated by the State of Mississippi to transport, house and care for the twenty-five young women victims of the Biloxi, Mississippi sex trafficking; and to protect the rights and sovereignty of the fourteen American Indian women, plus provide the absolute privacy and protection for the eleven non-American Indian women.

Our plan and invitation provides for complete protection from all unauthorized persons due to the location of the housing and medical facilities being on sovereign land of a federally acknowledged and recognized Indian Tribe, on land held-in-trust by the United States Department of Interior on behalf of the Mississippi Band of Choctaw Indians. In addition, security will be provided by sovereign security provided by the eleven federally acknowledged and recognized Indian Tribes under the auspices of the Bureau of Indian Affairs and the United States Department of Interior.

The concern of the tribal leaders is the loss of sovereign rights of the fourteen American Indian women, and the inability of any state-owned or operated facility to effectively house and protect these women, the medical professionals, their legal representatives, and their visiting family members. The likelihood of months of rehabilitation, recuperation and potential need to perform as witnesses in numerous trials is of utmost concern.

Following two hours of discussions and interruptions for phone calls, a resolution to affect the plan is passed with each of the eleven tribes with the Bureau of Indian Affairs in agreement.

Within an hour, a copy of the resolution is sent from the Office of the Department of Interior to key United States legislators, the Governor of Mississippi, and the President of the United States.

 At nine-twenty p.m., Eastern Standard Time, the Director of the Department of Interior is directed by Presidential Executive Order to take control of the care and protection of the twenty-five women named in accordance with the resolution provided by the eleven tribes. The order further states that is to be as soon as practical, but within twenty-four hours, and to provide housing and care on the sovereign Indian land within forty-eight hours.

*   *   *

While walking out to the bench at the end of the Hotel's Mark Twain Courtyard, I realize how great my life is and what a great day I've had. The six-o'clock evening news had the same information as the noon news regarding my ex-Ocean Springs home and 'Nancy Cole' plus the awesome news regarding the takeover by the tribes.

I'm reflecting on my day while enjoying my glass of chardonnay and watching the river busy with tugboats, ocean freighters and the dinner cruise on the Steamboat Natchez. I smile and remind myself, that's where I'll be tomorrow night, on the steamboat engulfed in the music and atmosphere of the Dixieland band, New Orleans style. Who knows, maybe I'll meet my man. The next two hours drift by as I enjoy a few more glasses of chardonnay and the incredible evening boat show. I'll sleep deep tonight.

*   *   *

At dusk in Cherokee, North Carolina on Qualla Grounds, a small group quietly and secretly celebrate with Native American prayers and songs, thanking the Creator for providing Alex with great strengths, bravery and wisdom. Once again, Alex's Mother learns about the incredible mission and silently prays for her daughter as tears fill her eyes and her lips tremble. Again, she cannot share the news with anyone.

About the Author

James A. McGregor is a Florida-based writer with careers in the oil, banking and finance, and casino industries. McGregor served six years in the U.S. Navy, with service in United States, Italy, and Malta. He also has extensive work experience with North American Indian Tribes. His banking and finance industry experience includes being the youngest person to serve as President-CEO of a Florida-based bank, and several years as a financial advisor for Wall Street based firms.

Mr. McGregor's current efforts include the creation, writing and publishing of the 'Alex, Cherokee Assassin' fiction series. In addition, his work includes assisting Indian tribes petitioning to the Bureau of Indian Affairs for federal acknowledgment. Much of the scope of his current work is available on his blog site www.casinotesracinotes.com

The 'Alex, Cherokee Assassin' fiction series includes a number of aspects and facets of McGregor's extensive work and travel experiences. Each 'Alex' story takes place in a major southeastern city; features retribution or vengeance for an unpunished crime against Native American tribes, people or persons; includes a casino gaming element; and uses Native American weapons to carry out each mission.